CHICKEN FOOT FARM

ANNE ESTEVIS

PIÑATA
BOOKS

PIÑATA BOOKS
ARTE PÚBLICO PRESS
HOUSTON, TEXAS

Chicken Foot Farm is funded in part by grants from the City of Houston through the Houston Arts Alliance and by the Exemplar Program, a program of Americans for the Arts in collaboration with the LarsonAllen Public Services Group, funded by the Ford Foundation.

Piñata Books are full of surprises!

Piñata Books
An imprint of
Arte Público Press
University of Houston
452 Cullen Performance Hall
Houston, Texas 77204-2004

Cover design by Giovanni Mora
Cover art by Joe Lopez

Estevis, Anne.
    Chicken Foot Farm / by Anne Estevis.
        p.   cm.
    Summary: Alejandro grows from ten years old to the age of seventeen, learning about life from his extended Mexican-American family on a small ranch in 1940s South Texas.
    ISBN 978-1-55885-505-2 (alk. paper)
    1. Mexican Americans—Juvenile fiction. [1. Mexican Americans—Fiction. 2. Ranch life—Texas—Fiction. 3. Family life—Texas—Fiction. 4. Texas—History—20th century—Fiction.] I. Title.
PZ7.E7498Ch 2008
[Fic]—dc22   2007048338
                                                                        CIP

8 9 0 1 2 3 4 5 6 7   10 9 8 7 6 5 4 3 2 1

Contents

Chicken Foot Farm is dedicated to Francisco, a good husband and a trusted critic, who inspires me to do something with my stories other than just talk about them.

I

Little Chicken Feet

Chicken Foot Farm was the nickname given to our land after an incident happened one stormy day when I was about seven years old. It occurred at the end of summer when the days are usually humid and hot in deep South Texas. I had climbed up into the fresno tree to see if there were any eggs in a grackle's nest. My mother was nearby in the large chicken yard. I sat in the tree and watched her as she tended to her chickens. She was tall and slender with long black hair that she wore pulled back in a bun. Her homemade dresses were usually kept covered with aprons in which she always tucked dainty handkerchiefs edged in lace that she had made herself.

Mamá looked up at me and beckoned for me to come down. "Alejandro, bring a bucket and help me gather my *pollitos*. There's a wicked-looking storm coming, and I don't want the chicks to drown."

Mamá gave her poultry a lot of attention and in return we always had chickens and eggs to eat. When she sold eggs and chickens, she hid the money in a lard can that she kept on top of her chifforobe. We all knew it was there.

"*Mi'jo*, hurry!" Mamá was struggling with her apron that was sagging from the weight of the chicks that she had already collected.

1

I knew what needed to be done because I had helped her on a number of stormy occasions to gather the tiny little chickens and place them in the big galvanized tub in the bathhouse. Mamá always placed a piece of old chenille bedspread in the bottom of the tub to keep the chicks comfortable until it was safe to put them back out on the ground.

Just as the wind began to whip the dust across the family compound, I jumped to the ground and grabbed one of several buckets that sat by the bathhouse door. I hurried to where Mamá was gathering chicks. A low rumbling caused me to shiver. I was afraid of the lightning that usually follows thunder, so I hurried to carry out my task.

I had gathered several chicks into the bucket when I saw Tía Inocencia rushing toward me. My aunt was married to my father's brother Erasmo, and they lived in a little house not far from ours. Tía Inocencia's ill-fitting shoes made a flip-flopping sound as she moved them quickly along the ground.

"Leave my chickens alone!" she screamed as she picked up one of the chicks I had already captured. "Where are you taking these chicks? Why are you stealing them?" She looked at me really mean-like, and I saw her bottom lip quiver.

Alarmed, I turned toward Mamá.

"Look, Inocencia, there's a storm coming," Mamá calmly said. She walked over to stand just a few inches in front of Tía Inocencia and looked sternly down at the short robust woman. "We need to protect all of the chicks."

"Oh, no, Ramona, you just want the biggest and best ones for yourself." Tía Inocencia grabbed at the batch of chicks huddled in Mamá's apron. Her shoes flipped and flopped, and one fell off.

"Believe me, Inocencia. I know my chicks from yours. I don't want yours at all. I just want to protect our investment," Mamá said.

"Well, I don't believe you!" Tía Inocencia yelled, the spittle flying out of her mouth.

Thunder roared, and I saw a streak of lightening flash across a darkening southeastern sky. A few drops of rain formed muddy dollops on the dusty ground around us. Mamá said nothing but bent down and released the chicks from her apron. She turned and went quickly into our house. I started to follow her, but she came right back out with her hand in her apron pocket. She immediately returned to where Tía Inocencia was attempting to tighten the strap of her floppy shoe.

Mamá reached down and swooped up a fluffy yellow chick. "This one is mine."

"It is not!" said Tía Inocencia. "It's mine! Here's one of yours!" She handed Mamá a skinny, scruffy-looking chick. "And this one's yours, and that one's yours." Tía Inocencia indicated by pointing with pursed lips and a jutting chin to several other rather poor-looking little *pollitos*.

"And you're sure this one is mine?" Mamá held out the scruffy chick that Tía Inocencia had given her.

Tía Inocencia slightly smiled. "Oh, yes. That one is definitely yours."

Mamá held the chick against her breast and splayed its left foot between her thumb and index finger. With her free hand she pulled a pair of small scissors from her apron pocket and quickly cut off the end of the chick's shortest toe. The chick let out a string of staccato peeps, and Mamá pressed tightly on the toe stump to suppress the bleeding.

"*¡Válgame Dios!* Ramona, what are you doing?" Tía Inocencia asked with a startled look on her face.

Mamá stood erect and looked squarely at Tía Inocencia. "I'm marking my chicks."

Tía Inocencia waited a few seconds before responding. "How brutal you are!" She pushed back two strands of oily hair that had fallen over her face and frowned at Mamá. "And how do I know you won't cheat me? How do I know you won't cut the toes off of my chicks, too? Can you please tell me that?"

"*Por que yo soy* Martínez. That's why," Mamá responded and put the peeping chick in my bucket. "*Yo soy* Martínez."

I really didn't know what Mamá meant by telling people that she was a Martínez. She usually said that when she seemed angry or hurt. She didn't need to say it because we all knew that indeed she was a Martínez. After all, she was Marcos Martínez's oldest daughter.

Tía Inocencia placed her hands on her hips. "Ramona, give me those scissors and let me mark my chicks. It's better to leave yours unmarked. That way I'll know for sure you're not cheating me."

"Absolutely not," Mamá answered and shook the scissors in Tía Inocencia's face. "The deed has already begun. I've marked my first chick. You said it was *my* chick. Now show me the rest of my *pollitos,* and I'll mark them too."

And so, as the rain began to fall on the compound, Tía Inocencia gathered all of the skinny and scruffy chicks and brought them to my mother who unabashedly cut off the ends of the shortest toes of their left feet. I think Tía Inocencia told all of the family members, and even some of the neighbors, what Mamá had done to the chicks' toes. She also complained that Mamá was cheating her, so she had Tío Erasmo build her a separate poultry yard for her chickens. It wasn't long after that incident that Mamá's skinny, scruffy chicks became handsome pullets. Tía Inocencia's chicks didn't do as well, and they soon became skinny and sick-looking pullets. Abuela Luciana said that someone had put a hex, like the evil eye, on Tía Inocencia's chickens. Abuelo Angel said that Tía Inocencia didn't know how to raise poultry and shouldn't have separated her chickens from Mamá's. My grandparents usually didn't agree on the evil eye issue.

Soon after that someone jokingly called our place Chicken Foot Farm, and the name stuck. Whenever any of us sold or killed a chicken, we always checked to see if it was missing the end of its little toe on the left foot. Mamá's chicken business thrived, and the lard can on top of the chifforobe always held money. Tía Inocencia seemed to lose interest in the endeavor. In time, all of the chickens on our farm were missing part of their little toes on their left feet.

II

Shadow Play

"Hey, Alejandro! Come try some of my delicious chicken," Cuco Briones, one of Papá's seasonal workers, called to me one evening.

As he smiled at me, I could see his long white teeth shining through his bushy mustache. I walked over to his campfire near the equipment shed where he and the other seasonal workers lived while they were employed by Papá.

From his large cast-iron kettle, Cuco removed some pieces of what he had just called chicken. "I tell you, *chamaco*, you are a good worker for being just a boy."

I had worked in the field all day alongside my brother Miguel and my sister Rosa. We younger children usually helped by hoeing weeds, picking cotton, and working in the vegetable harvests. Virginia, being the eldest girl, helped Mamá and Abuela Luciana in the house and kitchen.

Cuco took a piece of the chicken, wrapped it in a tortilla, and, with a big grin, gave it to me. "Your father must be very proud of you."

I didn't want to tell Cuco how hard I tried to please him, but Papá seldom said much to me unless I did something wrong. Papá seemed especially proud of my oldest brother, Ernesto, and I had heard Papá tell Ernesto many times that he was a good son and that someday all of Papá's land would be his.

I finished the tasty taco and stayed standing beside Cuco's campfire hoping for another.

"Here, eat more so you can grow up strong and be a farmer like your father." Cuco offered me another taco.

I wanted to be a farmer, but I also wanted to grow up to be like Ernesto who was a good brother to me. He was patient and kind, taught me many things, and even helped me with my school homework.

I took the second taco. "*Gracias.* Yes, I do want to be a farmer." I thought of how Miguel had told me that he didn't want to grow crops but preferred to work in an office or a store. I couldn't understand why Miguel felt that way.

As I was eating my second taco, my nosy sister Rosa came rushing over to Cuco's campfire, probably thinking she was being left out of our little feast.

"Do you want some chicken too, *muchacha*?" Cuco asked Rosa.

The smile on Rosa's face faded as she looked down into Cuco's kettle. "That doesn't look like chicken!" she said to Cuco. "What kind of chicken is that?"

"It's *tlacuache*," he answered, "and it's delicious!" He laughed and rubbed his fat round belly.

"Opossum! Yuck! Don't eat that, Alejandro!" Rosa shook her head vigorously, and her two colorfully festooned braids whipped about her shoulders.

It was too late. I had already eaten the tasty pieces of marsupial. Rosa began pushing me toward the kitchen with her usual demeanor that indicated that she was in charge. Although she was small, she was muscular and strong, no doubt a result of her being a big tomboy who would rather play outside with the boys than perform any type of domestic activity.

"Mamá says not to eat *tlacuaches*. They can give you a disease that makes you foam at the mouth. Hurry!" Rosa guided me into our kitchen and over to the enamel washbasin where she force-fed me a small piece of green Palmolive soap.

"Here, put some water in your mouth and swish it around," she demanded as she poured water into my mouth from a tin cup.

I couldn't swish because I was gagging on the soap. I coughed out the soap and proceeded to vomit up the entire contents of my stomach. All the while Rosa was scolding me as usual. It was really difficult for me to believe that she and Miguel were twins. He was quiet and withdrawn, and she was loud and pushy. But, thanks to Rosa, I didn't get the foaming mouth disease. When Mamá heard about the incident, including what Rosa had done to me, she told me nicely not to eat any more of Cuco's "chicken." I didn't eat with him again, but I did spend many evenings after chores with him. He taught me and Miguel to play dominoes. That was fun, and we played a lot.

Some of the farmworkers could play the guitar, and when they did, Cuco would sing and dance around the campfires. His big white teeth glistened in the firelight, and his fat belly bounced in time with the music. He seemed to enjoy performing for us. Sometimes he would take my little cousin Roque and put Roque's feet on top of his so that the little boy was standing on Cuco's big work boots. Cuco would then take Roque by the hands and the two would dance around the campfire while Cuco sang this haunting nonsense song:

Jara jara jumba, jumba, jumba.
Jara jara jumba, jumba, ja!

Cuco would twirl around and around until Roque could no longer keep his footing on top of Cuco's big work boots. The two of them would usually fall down on the ground and roll around laughing. Miguel, my cousin Cándido, and I would join them on the ground. We would laugh and giggle until all of us would get the hiccups.

The most fun I ever had with Cuco was making movies, as he called it. It started one evening just before dark when Cuco saw Miguel, Rosa, and me sitting under the fresno tree cleaning the mud off of the wheels of the *carretilla* that Abuelo Angel used to haul things around the compound.

"*Oigan, chamacos,* want to make movies?" Cuco asked as he approached us with his big grin.

Of course we did, and we all said so at the same time.

"Well, one of you go into the house and borrow a kerosene lamp from your mother. And bring a big white bedsheet."

That being quickly done, Cuco hung the sheet on the clothesline. Then he told us to sit down in front of the sheet as if it were a movie screen. Cuco went behind the sheet and placed the lighted lamp on an empty fruit crate. He placed his chubby hands in front of the lamp so that their shadows fell on the sheet. He formed his hands and fingers into an animal with a long muzzle.

"Grrrrr. I'm going to eat you up," Cuco said as he moved his hands around in front of the lamp pretending that his hands were a bloodthirsty animal.

We children laughed and screamed and asked for more, except for Roque who started crying because he was afraid of the animal that Cuco's hands made. Mamá and my sister, Virginia, came outside to see what the commotion was. They stayed to join in the fun.

In time, we became good at forming all kinds of animals. The girls usually made birds and butterflies, but we boys made dogs, rabbits, eagles, and ferocious animals and monsters that tried to eat each other. Virginia and Rosa added props and story lines to their repertory, which gave new dimensions to our moviemaking. Some nights we put on shadow movies for others in the compound, including the hired workers. Roque, as he became braver, would run up to the sheet and attempt to hit the shadow animals. Even Papá seemed to enjoy our efforts, and he would clap and laugh and shout, "*¡Bravo! ¡Bravo!*" I was so very happy that we pleased him.

One night some lawmen came to Chicken Foot Farm while Rosa, Miguel, and I were setting up the bedsheet and kerosene lamp for an evening of fun. I was the first one to see the big man with a metal star on his chest as he stepped into the light of the lamp. There was another man following a little distance behind him. Both men wore white hats.

"I need to see Sigifredo Balderas," the big man said.

Before any of us could respond, Ernesto stepped out of our house and said, "My father is in bed very sick. Can I help you?"

It was true that Papá was sick and was in bed. He had had a fever and chills all day. Mamá had bathed him with rubbing alcohol, and when that was all gone, she used Tío Balde's whiskey on Papá.

"Can I help you?" Ernesto repeated.

"No, son. You tell your father to come out here, or we're coming in to get him." The big man stepped closer to Ernesto who turned and reentered the house.

A minute or two later, Papá appeared at the door looking disheveled and unsteady on his feet.

"Come on out here," the big man commanded.

Papá slowly stepped on to the porch, holding on to the screen door for support. Both lawmen rushed forward and grabbed Papá by the upper arms and dragged him into the yard.

"Where is Cuco Briones?" the big man demanded.

"I don't know. I haven't seen him today," Papá said. He moistened his dried lips with his tongue and looked the big man in the face.

"This one is drunk," the big man said to his partner. "He smells of cheap whiskey."

The men turned loose of Papá's arms, and he slumped down to the ground. At that, Mamá, who had been standing in the doorway, came bursting out of the house.

"*¡Ay, Dios mío!* My poor husband is sick! He's not drunk!" she screamed.

The big man did not flinch although Mamá walked right up to him with her nostrils flaring.

"Tell your husband that I will be back when he sobers up and can remember where Cuco Briones has gone."

The two men left, and Ernesto and Mamá helped my shaken papá back to bed. Our shadow movies were ruined for the night as we were too frightened to stay outside for fear the men with white hats would come back.

Cuco Briones never returned to Chicken Foot Farm. I never heard what terrible thing he had done to cause the lawmen to pursue him. If Papá knew, he never told me. Sometimes I would think of Cuco running from the big man with the star on his chest. More often I thought of Cuco Briones, with his white teeth glistening through his bushy mustache, as he danced around his campfire singing:

> *Jara jara jumba, jumba, jumba.*
> *Jara jara jumba, jumba, ja!*

III

La Mano Pachona

M y parents wanted us children to be virtuous individuals, so they saw that we received some sort of religious education. At about the age of nine I began what we called catechism classes at the parish church under the direction of Father Casimiro. Every Wednesday night Papá or one of my uncles would drive me to and from the church for my classes.

One particular night, an addendum to Father Casimiro's lesson left a lasting impression on me. He told the class about a demon named Satan who lived down in the center of the earth in a place called Hell, and if we were bad children, Satan could reach up through the ground and grab us by the feet. If he wished, Satan could pull us down through the dirt and into Hell to live with him. Father Casimiro paced back and forth before us as he delivered this information. Finally, he ceased talking and walked over and stopped directly in front of me.

"So be careful, children, because if you are bad, Satan can reach right up out of the ground and drag you down to Hell with him."

I looked up at Father Casimiro. He was looking at me and frowning. I looked away from his gaze and wondered why he had chosen me for his finale. What had I done? I quickly took inventory of my actions of the past week and could think of nothing remarkable.

That night at home I was rather quiet and pensive. When I needed to go out to the separate sleeping house that I shared with my brothers, I found that I was afraid to go alone. My thoughts were on Satan and his uncanny ability to reach up through the packed earth and grab a child by the foot. I finally got Ernesto to accompany me. The next night I told Mamá that I was afraid to go outside alone.

"My goodness, Alejandro, you're not a little boy anymore. You always go outside by yourself. What's wrong with you?" she said.

I burst out crying. When I calmed down, I told her about Father Casimiro's description of how Satan pulls children down to Hell.

Mamá seemed surprised and replied, "That can't be true. Satan doesn't do that. He can't do that."

On the next Wednesday night Mamá had Tío Balde, Papá's youngest brother, drive us to the church where she point-blank asked Father Casimiro, "Did you tell Alejandro that Satan could reach up through the ground and grab him by the foot?"

The priest scratched his head, looked at me, and replied, "Yes, something to that effect."

"Now Father, tell me, do you really think that it is physically possible for Satan to do that?" Mamá asked.

"Well, I suppose that Satan can do anything he wants to do," Father Casimiro said.

"Do you know of anyone that has had that done to them by Satan? If you do, I want their names," said Mamá.

"Now, now, Ramona, don't get so upset about this. I tell that story to all the children so they'll be good," said Father Casimiro. He smiled down at me and laid his hand on the top of my head.

Mamá looked Father Casimiro directly in the eyes and said, "I think that is a terrible thing to teach children just to make them obedient. Now Alejandro is afraid to go outside alone after dark because of what you have told him."

"Well, Ramona, how else can we make children behave?" asked Father Casimiro as he removed his hand from my head.

"I'll tell you how. By ensuring that they receive rewards for their good deeds and punishment for the bad ones," said Mamá.

I didn't stay for class that night. In fact, Mamá refused to send me back to Father Casimiro's catechism classes. I was fifteen years old before I finally took my first Holy Communion. But that wasn't the end of the Satan story.

Several weeks after I dropped out of catechism classes, Abuela Luciana asked Rosa to go over to Madama Fisher's house to borrow a spool of red thread. The Fishers lived about a quarter of a mile down the road from our farm. Rosa asked me to go with her. I happily consented as I loved going into Madama Fisher's house and seeing all of the interesting things she had.

When we arrived at Madama's house, we knocked at the kitchen door as usual. Madama invited us into her kitchen. Something smelled good. The aroma was coming from a big platter of chicken sitting on the table. It was fried chicken, and each piece had a thick brown crust. Mamá and Abuela Luciana cooked chicken in many ways. They prepared chicken *caldo*, chicken *tamales*, chicken *en mole*, chicken *pipián*, and chicken *con arroz*. But absolutely never did they prepare fried chicken. I had eaten fried chicken at Madama Fisher's house several times, and it was always tasty. And now, I was standing just a few feet from a platter of fried chicken and was pondering its delicious taste.

Rosa told Madama what Abuela Luciana needed to borrow, and Madama walked out of the kitchen to go get the spool of thread. I saw that Rosa was occupied with petting Madama's large white Persian cat. I quickly took a chicken leg from the platter and stuffed it down in my overall pocket just as Madama returned with the thread.

We said good-bye, exited the kitchen, and started down the road. It was almost dark, so I took a chance that Rosa wouldn't see the chicken leg that I pulled out of my pocket. I began devouring it.

"What are you eating? You better not have stolen a piece of Madama's chicken," Rosa said as she grabbed at my arm.

I hurried on a little ahead of Rosa. "Madama usually gives me something to eat. She would have given me this chicken leg," I answered as I finished off the last of the meat and began sucking on the end of the bone.

Just then something caught my feet and caused me to trip. I dropped the chicken bone. I jumped up and attempted to run. Something held fast to both of my feet. I thought that Satan had grabbed me. I began to scream with fright as I hobbled and hopped along the road toward home.

Rosa began running, yelling for someone to help me. Ernesto must have heard her because he started coming down the road calling out to us. By the time I got myself loose from Satan's grasp, Ernesto had reached me.

"What's wrong?" Ernesto asked.

I could hardly talk because of my crying and sobbing.

Finally I was able to say, "Satan caught my foot and tried to pull me down to Hell."

Ernesto put his arm around my shoulders and began walking me home. Rosa didn't wait for us to get home before she began her tattling about what had just happened.

"Satan should take him straight to Hell. Ernesto, you will never guess what our little brother did. He stole chicken from Madama."

"He stole a chicken?" I don't see a chicken," Ernesto said.

"Not a chicken. A piece of Madama's fried chicken, from her table," explained Rosa.

By this time we had reached our yard. Mamá and Tía Inocencia were waiting outside for us. Ernesto guided me into the midst of the women who were curious to know what all the yelling was about. Then Ernesto disappeared. Mamá herded us into the house. Of course, Rosa didn't wait to repeat the story about me stealing the piece of chicken. She reported that I tried to sneak away from Madama's house, but I kept falling down.

"Satan grabbed my feet and tried to pull me down to Hell," I explained.

Mamá looked sternly at me. "I'm disappointed to hear that you stole something from Madama Fisher."

I was confused. Why was Mamá more concerned about a little piece of chicken and not about Satan attacking me?

"Mamá, Satan grabbed me!" I cried.

Tía Inocencia narrowed her eyes and frowned at me. "That wasn't Satan. That was *la mano pachona*," she said, with her usual air of a know-it-all.

"What do you mean by *la mano pachona*?" Rosa asked. "A hairy hand?"

"It's the hand that can grab you when you've done something naughty, as Alejandro did tonight," said Tía Inocencia. She lowered her voice and said, "So you children had better be good, or *la mano pachona* will get you."

"Here's your *mano pachona*," said Ernesto holding something up for us to see.

It was a tangle of wire.

"Alejandro got his feet caught in this mess. That's why he had trouble walking. I found it on the road at the place where he was hopping around," Ernesto said.

"Well, I still say that Alejandro had better watch out for *la mano pachona*. It will grab naughty children," warned Tía Inocencia as she shook her fat finger at me.

"I don't agree with you, Inocencia," Mamá said curtly. "I think if Alejandro does something naughty, then he needs to watch out for *me!*" Mamá walked to the front door and lit a lantern. She went out the doorway motioning for me to follow her. We walked quickly down the road and soon arrived at Madama Fisher's house, where I was required to confess to Madama and to plead for her forgiveness.

"And, Madama," Mamá said, "Alejandro will pay for the chicken leg by working for you from sunup to sundown for the next two Saturdays. Anything you need done. The harder the work, the better."

"Oh, my goodness, Ramona, that's not necessary," said Madama Fisher, and she looked at me and smiled.

"It *is* necessary," replied Mamá.

"But it was just a little piece of chicken," insisted Madama Fisher.

"A piece of chicken today, a diamond ring tomorrow. Who knows what it might be by next week?" said Mamá.

I worked for Madama Fisher for the next two Saturdays. I don't know if there ever was a demon named Satan that could reach up through the ground and grab children and pull them down to Hell. As far as *la mano pachona*, I don't know if there was really one of those either. I do know, however, that there was someone who had tremendous control over my behavior. Her name was Mamá.

IV

Muggy Dan

"Look, Virginia, she's got a grandfather clock." Abuela Luciana was looking out the window at the farmhouse across the road from Chicken Foot Farm.

"Let me see," Virginia responded and quickly moved to the window to look at the furniture being unloaded from a big red farm truck.

The farmhouse and the red truck belonged to Madama Fisher. She had recently hired a man named Mr. McIlroy to help with the work on her large farm, and he and his family were now moving into the vacant house. Although I was cleaning the storage shed that hot June morning, I took a number of breaks to watch and listen as the new neighbors took boxes and furniture into the house.

I was lonely without Miguel and Rosa who had gone with Mamá to visit her parents in San Antonio. I hoped the new family would have some children, especially boys. I watched as things were brought out of the truck, but I never saw any boys, only a skinny redheaded girl.

For several days after the McIlroys moved in, I climbed the chinaberry tree in the front yard and watched the redheaded girl as she explored her new yard and played on her large front porch. From time to time her mother would call out to her to come inside. I wanted to see the girl and especially her curly red hair a little closer, so I moved the milk stool out to the barrow ditch in front of our house and sat there watching her from behind the tall grass.

Soon the girl noticed me and yelled "Hello!"

This startled me, so I quickly looked the other way. She yelled again, and I couldn't help but look at her. She was motioning for me to come over. I jumped up and ran to the back of our house.

Abuela Luciana had witnessed all of this. "Alejandro, why don't you go across the road and talk to the little girl? Ask her what her name is."

"I already know her name. I've heard her mother calling her."

"That's good. Your father and grandpa have already talked to the new neighbors and your grandpa said they are nice people." Abuela Luciana turned away to continue sweeping the floor. Then she stopped her broom and said, "Go invite the little girl to come over here, and I'll make *horchata* for the two of you."

I loved *horchata,* and I was willing to overcome my shyness for a glass of that delicious drink. I walked across the road. There were a number of toys and other items scattered around on the front porch, but the little girl was nowhere in sight. I searched all around the yard without finding her. I thought of the *horchata.* That gave me the courage to go to the McIlroy's front door and knock. The girl's mother came to the door.

"Can Muggy Dan come out and play?" I asked.

The woman apparently did not understand me. "Who are you looking for?"

"Muggy Dan." I said.

The woman smiled. "Are you saying *Muggy Dan?*"

"Yes. Muggy Dan," I responded.

The redheaded girl quickly stepped in front of her mother and held the screen door slightly open. "Hello. Why didn't you come over when I called? Didn't you hear me?" she asked.

I ignored her questions and pointed across the road toward the compound. "Abuela wants to know if you want to come drink *horchata* at my house?"

The girl nodded and grinned, showing that she lacked some of her teeth. I also noticed that her skin was covered with tiny brown spots. I couldn't stop looking at her. She was fascinating. I had never seen a person like this.

Muggy Dan's mother opened the screen door wider. "Why don't you come in and have a Coney Island with us? Then my daughter can go drink *horchata* with you."

Mrs. McIlroy was a soft-spoken woman, and she seemed friendly toward me. I gladly went in and sat down at the kitchen table. The kitchen was inside their house and not a separate building like ours. Mrs. McIlroy gave me a full bottle of Dr. Pepper, something I seldom got at my house. Next, she placed before me a small plate that held a wiener in a long bun with chili and cheese on top. I had never eaten a Coney Island before, and it was good. This was the first of many new food items that I would eventually eat that summer while sitting in Mrs. McIlroy's kitchen. Among the new foods that I would be served were chicken pot pies and hot cakes with melted butter and Log Cabin syrup. When the syrup tins, which looked like little cabins, were emptied, Mrs. McIlroy washed and dried them for us. All summer we made little towns out of the Log Cabin tins on Muggy Dan's front porch.

The new experience with the Coney Island made me forget about the *horchata,* and after we had finished eating our first meal together, Muggy Dan and I went out to her front porch. The porch was large and shaded, and on it were lots of things that looked interesting to me. I began touching some of the objects.

"Here, you can play with these." Muggy Dan offered me a ball and some jacks.

I didn't take them. Rosa played with those things. I was more interested in Muggy Dan's big coloring book and a cigar box containing Crayola crayons.

"You can't play with my little dishes or my stove or my doll's buggy. And you sure can't touch Shirley." Muggy Dan picked up a Shirley Temple doll out of a pink wicker doll buggy. "She and I have dresses just alike, only mine is getting too small."

I didn't want to touch any of her stupid girl stuff, and I was too old to play with most of her toys anyway. "Can I color in your coloring book?"

"You can only color the page that I tell you to color." Muggy Dan pushed the cigar box toward me and began flipping through the pages of the coloring book. She found a suitable one and gave it to me. "And, don't you dare break any of my crayons, and stay inside the lines."

We spent most of the afternoon on her front porch. She had a game called Parcheesi that she taught me how to play. It was fun, but I liked the crayons and coloring book best. I was coloring a picture of a dog when I thought about the *horchata*. I left without saying anything to Muggy Dan. She was busy changing Shirley's clothing and softly singing about some cowboys sitting around a fire. One of the cowboys wanted to see his mother, but he was dying. I thought Muggy Dan's song was weird, and I thought she was weird too.

Early the next afternoon, Muggy Dan, pushing Shirley in the doll buggy, came to our house and asked me to come out and play with her.

"Can we go see the animals?" She pointed toward the corral where Papá's two mules were kept.

"Sure, come on." I ran ahead of her.

Muggy Dan wrinkled up her nose when we neared the corral. "It stinks here. What other animals do you have?"

"We have a milk cow, dogs, cats, and chickens. We have lots of chickens."

"You have a cow? I want to see the cow."

"She's staked out by the irrigation ditch grazing on the tall grass. You can see her later." I couldn't imagine why she wanted to see our cow. I looked at the brown spots on Muggy Dan's face. "Can I touch you?" I reached toward her.

"What do you mean 'touch me'?" She stepped back from me, and I saw a look of defensiveness on her face.

"Your arm, that's all. I just want to feel those bumps."

"You're crazy! I don't have any bumps." She held out an arm to me.

I felt the skin on her arm and it didn't feel unusual at all. It felt like regular skin. I was disappointed. "Why do you have so many brown spots on your skin? Don't they bother you?"

"My mother says they're beauty marks. So there!" Muggy Dan withdrew her freckled arm.

I ignored her response. "Let's go ask Abuela to make us *horchata.*"

Before we found Abuela Luciana, Abuelo Angel called out to me. He motioned for me and Muggy Dan to come over to where he was sitting in his old wooden chair under the fresno tree. He held something in his gnarled and knobby fingers.

"Look what I've made for you. Telephones." He held up two empty tin cans. He had punched holes in the bottom of the cans and connected them with a long twine tied to pieces of wooden matches that he had pushed through the holes. "You each take a can and stretch out the twine. You can hear each other talking through the cans."

Muggy Dan and I tried it, and it worked. We walked and talked all over Chicken Foot Farm, and then we took our telephones to Muggy Dan's house to show her mother. Mrs. McIlroy came outside and talked to us on the telephones.

Muggy Dan went into her house and quickly returned with a large ball of twine. "Let's make the telephones longer so you can talk to me from your house. We'll run the twine across the road."

She and I quickly added new twine and stretched our telephones across the road. It didn't seem to work as well now. We were standing with the cans stretched between us when I saw Toribio Tovar's pickup truck approaching.

"Let go! Put your can down," I yelled to Muggy Dan.

"No! You put yours down first!"

We stood at an impasse as Toribio's truck came nearer.

"Let go of the can! That truck is going to hit the twine!" I expected her to at least lower her can.

But Muggy Dan held the can up to her ear. I should have done something sooner, but I didn't. The front of Toribio's truck had barely touched the twine when Muggy Dan and I let go at the same time. Toribio waved at me and continued on down the road pulling our telephones along with him.

Muggy Dan screamed at me. "Look what you did, dummy! You ruined our telephones!"

This made me angry. "*You* did it, *sonsa*! I told you to let go! Why didn't you let go?"

"Because *you* didn't let go!" She wheeled around and went into her house.

That evening Mamá, Rosa, and Miguel arrived home from San Antonio. I told Miguel about the redheaded girl who had moved into the house across the road. I described her brown spots and related how she had ruined the telephones that Abuelo Angel had made. Miguel didn't appear very interested in hearing about Muggy Dan. He seemed more occupied with the books and model airplanes that he had brought home. He had gotten them from Abuelo Marcos's mercantile store.

"That little girl is *muy mandona*, so bossy, and now that you're home, I promise I won't play with her anymore," I told Miguel. I broke my promise the next day when Muggy Dan came over pushing Shirley Temple in the pink buggy. I guess I still found the little redheaded girl fascinating.

V

Chinaberries

It was a few days before Labor Day, and summer vacation from school was almost over. Miguel and Rosa were going to attend junior high for the first time, and I didn't like the thought of being left behind in elementary school.

"Who am I going to eat lunch with?" I asked. Miguel and I always took just one paper bag with bean tacos for both of us.

"You can take your own lunch and eat with your friends," Miguel answered.

I frowned. "What friends?"

"You have a special friend across the road," Miguel said and laughed.

"*Mentiroso*, you're a liar. Muggy Dan's not my friend. I don't even like that bossy little girl."

Miguel said nothing more and returned to the model airplane he was assembling. I went outside feeling rather unsure of how I was going to survive not having Miguel in the same school with me. I saw Muggy Dan coming around the side of our house pushing her doll buggy.

"Hello. Look who I brought to visit you." Muggy Dan smiled her somewhat toothless grin and stopped the buggy.

I looked at her but said nothing.

"See? It's Shirley in her new jumper just like mine."
Muggy Dan pushed the buggy over to where I was standing.

I peered into the buggy and saw that Shirley Temple had on
some clothing that resembled what Muggy Dan was wearing.

"My mother made these outfits for us." She picked up the
doll and held it out in front of her so I could see their clothing
better.

"Yes, I see what you're talking about." I tried not to seem
interested.

Muggy Dan placed the doll back in the buggy. "Can we go
see the mules and the cow?" She pointed out toward the corral.

I looked toward the corral and then beyond. "No, let's go
to the *monte*," I suggested. I thought she would be afraid of the
large dark woods that grew about a quarter of a mile from
Chicken Foot Farm. I wanted to scare her. That would show her
how brave I was and how foolish she was.

"What's a *monte*?" she asked.

"You don't even know what a *monte* is?" I pointed to the
tall growth of *huisache*, mesquite, and *nopal*. "You'd better not
get scared or cry if we go in there because it's a real scary
place. There's even a *bruja* that lives in a little house in the
middle of the *monte*. She's a real mean witch."

"That's not true. Besides, I don't believe in witches. My
mother says there's no such thing."

Muggy Dan parked the doll buggy under the chinaberry
tree, and we began walking toward the *monte*. As we passed
our bathhouse I retrieved my *resortera* from the nail where I
had hung it that morning, and I put it in my pocket.

We crossed the already cleaned cotton field and arrived at
the edge of the large growth of trees and cacti.

I again warned Muggy Dan. "Don't forget that there's a
witch that lives in there."

"And you don't forget that there's no such thing." She hurried ahead of me.

We entered the *monte* on one of its narrow paths. I moved in front of her to lead the way. We had walked only a few minutes when there was a rustling in the brush ahead of us. I turned around and ran past Muggy Dan and didn't stop until I was well out of the *monte*. I expected to see her right behind me, but when I turned to look, she was nowhere in sight.

"Muggy Dan! Come on! Hurry!" I yelled. I did not want to go back for her. The thoughts of a large javalina eating her skinny freckled legs sent a shiver through my body. "Muggy Dan!"

"I'm coming," she called as she appeared at the edge of the *monte*.

She walked up to me and laughed. "It was two *chachalacas*. That's all." She didn't seem upset or scared.

This didn't set well with me, so I said, "It could have been a javalina or even the witch!"

"No, it wasn't either one of those. I said there were two *chachalacas*. I saw them."

"I don't think it could have been birds. There was too much noise in the brush." I was not going to give in. I was sure that it was something big like a javalina.

She stood standing with her hands on her hips looking at me. "Well, are we going back in the *monte*, or not?"

"Not with a javalina running around in there. I'm going back to my house." I walked away from Muggy Dan. I heard her following me.

We walked silently back to my yard. Muggy Dan picked up Shirley from the buggy under the chinaberry tree. She began singing to her doll softly. It was the song about the dying cowboy.

I reached up into the tree and picked several of the tree's hard round berries. I took my *resortera* from my back pocket. Ernesto had made me this little weapon from a Y-shaped tree branch. It was outfitted with two rubber straps attached to a leather piece. "Hey, watch what I can do."

Muggy Dan stopped singing, put Shirley back into the buggy, and looked at me. I placed a chinaberry in the leather piece attached to the rubber straps. I pulled back and aimed.

"See that bucket over there by the willow tree? Watch me hit it." I sighted carefully and let the chinaberry fly. I missed. "Wait. I'll do it again." I missed again.

Muggy Dan laughed loudly.

"It's because the straps are uneven. I'll have to fix them later." I didn't like that she had laughed at me.

I decided to test Muggy Dan's tree-climbing ability. "Let's climb the tree," I said as I kicked off my well-worn shoes and hurried up the chinaberry tree.

Muggy Dan pushed the buggy closer to the tree. "I don't want to take off my shoes. Besides, I might ruin my new jumper. I think I'll go home." She took hold of the buggy and began walking away. "I'll see you tomorrow, Alex."

"What did you call me?" I jumped down from the tree.

Muggy Dan stopped and turned toward me. "I called you Alex."

"That's not my name." I had never heard that name before, and I didn't like it. I couldn't understand why she was calling me something probably very bad. I reached up into the tree and picked two chinaberries. I loaded one into the leather piece of my *resortera*.

"Well, that's what my mother says your name is. Alex." Muggy Dan turned and began pushing Shirley toward the road.

She wasn't going to get by with this. I pulled back on the rubber straps and aimed at Muggy Dan. I let go of the chinaberry, and it hit her on the back of one of her legs. She let go of the buggy, grabbed her leg with her hand, and screamed. She didn't turn around. I reloaded my weapon and shot another chinaberry. This time I saw it hit her on her back. She took hold of the buggy handle and ran toward the road screeching very loudly. The back wheels of the buggy came off and rolled into our barrow ditch. Muggy Dan didn't stop, but plowed her way across the dirt road with the back axle of the pink wicker doll buggy. I felt I was more than justified by what had just happened.

That night Muggy Dan and her parents arrived at our kitchen. We were just finishing our evening meal when they were ushered in by Abuelo Angel and given places to sit at our long kitchen table. Abuela Luciana served the guests the perfunctory coffee and *pan dulce*. Papá and Mr. McIlroy, both wearing khaki shirts and khaki pants with bandannas hanging out of a back pocket, discussed cotton prices and bales per acre. Mamá showed Mrs. McIlroy the lace that she was making. Muggy Dan sat across the table wrinkling her nose at me every time I looked at her.

After the McIlroys had finished consuming their cups of coffee and sweet bread, Muggy Dan's mother addressed the purpose of their visit.

In a soft voice, Mrs. McIlroy slowly said, "I'm sorry to have to tell you that your son shot our daughter with chinaberries today." She pointed to a large red bump on the back of Muggy Dan's leg. Then she raised Muggy Dan's blouse and showed my parents a bigger and redder bump on her back.

Mamá gasped and covered her mouth with her pink batiste handkerchief. Papá stood up from the table and looked angrily down at me. "Why would you do such a thing to this little girl?"

I lowered my head. I heard Rosa stifle a giggle. No one else in the kitchen made a sound except for Abuela Luciana who was whispering one of her prayers and making the sign of the cross toward me.

In a loud voice, Papá said, "Why did you do this?"

"Papá, she called me a bad name," I meekly said without looking up.

"What bad name?"

"She called me Alex, and I don't like being called bad names."

My father didn't respond; he just stood looking at me. I was beginning to think that I might be in big trouble.

Mrs. McIlroy cleared her throat. "Pardon me for interrupting, but that's not a bad name. I'm sorry that you misunderstood. Alex is just a nickname for Alejandro."

I didn't understand. "But, that is not my name." I looked up, and everyone at the table was staring at me with puzzled looks on their faces with the exception of Abuela Luciana who was still praying for me. My throat tightened, and I was afraid that I was going to start crying. I lowered my head again.

Mrs. McIlroy softly said, "Think about this, Alejandro. You have been calling my daughter 'Muggy Dan' and that's not her name. Her name is Margaret Ann."

I was stunned. I looked at Muggy Dan who wrinkled her freckled nose at me.

Mrs. McIlroy continued, "She never got angry at you for giving her a nickname. So why would you get angry at her?"

I still didn't understand. I couldn't answer Mrs. McIlroy's question. Wasn't Muggy Dan the name I was hearing? That's what I was sure that I had heard Mrs. McIlroy calling her daughter.

My parents were humiliated to hear of my behavior, and they assured the McIlroys that I would be punished. After

Muggy Dan and her parents had gone home and the rest of the family had left the kitchen, my parents discussed my punishment while I sat at the table in silence. Finally, Mamá handed Papá a canister containing uncooked long grain rice.

I watched as my father walked to a corner in the kitchen and slowly poured some rice from his hand onto the linoleum rug that covered the dirt floor. As he spread the rice with the palm of his hand, he said, "As my father punished me when I was a child, I shall punish you."

He told me to take off my overalls. Then he had me kneel in my underwear in the corner with my knees on the rice. I was mortified, and I began crying quietly. Mamá and Papá stayed sitting behind me at the table saying nothing.

I don't know how long I remained kneeling on the rice. My knees began burning terribly, and I was to the point of begging Papá to let me get up when Abuelo Angel came into the kitchen. He told Papá that I had had enough punishment.

It would be a number of years before I fully realized the extent of the injustice that I had dealt Margaret Ann McIlroy. It became obvious to me in high school that Alex was indeed not a bad word. Many of my school friends began calling me Alex. Unfortunately, I never had the opportunity to apologize to Margaret Ann. Mr. McIlroy left Madama Fisher's employment soon after I shot Margaret Ann with the chinaberries. I heard the McIlroys had moved to Lubbock where Mr. McIlroy got a better paying job. To tell the truth, for a long time I missed that bossy redheaded girl.

VI

Night of the Almost Naked Dancer

Tío Balde, Papá's youngest brother, lived at home with my grandparents for many years. Because he wasn't much older than Ernesto, those two were more like brothers than like uncle and nephew. Mamá wasn't always happy that Ernesto liked to spend time with Tío Balde. She said that Tío Balde drank too much beer and was always talking about girls. He did seem to have lots of girlfriends, at least according to the stories he told us.

Another characteristic that Mamá didn't seem to appreciate in Tío Balde was his penchant for playing practical jokes on friends and family members. Mamá often complained to Papá. "Your brother is insensitive with the tricks he plays on people. I hope someone gets angry and makes him suffer for his mischief."

"*Déjalo*, he's just a young man having fun and enjoying life," Papá would answer and smile at Mamá.

Tío Balde spent a lot of evenings visiting Ernesto in the sleeping house where my brothers and I slept. He and Ernesto liked to talk, and they discussed many things, such as the weather, baseball, and pretty girls. Tío Balde would bring beer and cigarettes because he couldn't drink and smoke in my grandparents' house. That would have been very disrespectful.

Early one evening when Tío Balde was smoking and drinking out in the sleeping house, I overheard him telling Ernesto something about a spinster, Señorita Sinforosa, one of our nearest neighbors.

"I swear to you, Ernesto," Tío Balde said in a low voice. "I saw her turn herself into a beautiful young woman. I saw her dancing around a large black cauldron in her yard. And what's more, she was almost naked." He smiled and took a long draw on his cigarette, then glanced over to where Miguel and I were lying across the bed.

Ernesto looked at Tío Balde with an apparent look of puzzlement, but he said nothing. Señorita Sinforosa must have been eighty years old. She lived alone in her small house a little ways into the large *monte* that bordered our farm. In fact, the growth of *huisache* and mesquite trees was so tall and thick around her house that all we could see was just the peak of the roof.

Tío Balde looked again at Miguel and me, smiled and continued his story. "She was a beautiful young woman. The most beautiful I've ever seen." He opened another bottle of beer.

I wasn't even sure what Señorita Sinforosa looked like, but I certainly knew that she didn't look young or beautiful. The elderly woman didn't venture out much, and it was whispered by some of the neighborhood gossips that she was a witch. It was said that she had at least two dozen cats living at her place and that she could turn herself into a cat whenever she desired.

Because of these stories, I avoided going near Señorita Sinforosa's place, although the *monte* with its little paths leading into the darkness of the trees and bushes was inviting to me. But the idea of witches was frightening for me. I had not been back to the *monte* since the time Muggy Dan and I had ventured into it. I perked up when Tío Balde told Ernesto that Señorita

Sinforosa could turn herself into a beautiful, *naked* girl. Well, almost naked.

Ernesto laughed and said, *"Mentiroso."* He took a drink from Tío Balde's beer bottle. "You shouldn't be such a liar."

"I'm not lying. It's the truth." Tío Balde smiled at Miguel and me and continued, "Some of the *chavos* down at the *cantina* told me that she always does this when the moon is full. I didn't believe it myself until I saw it last night."

Miguel nudged me and whispered, "Listen to this *chismoso.*"

"And you say she danced around a *paila*, a black cauldron? Why would she do that?" Ernesto opened another bottle of beer for Tío Balde.

"Witches do that, but I don't know why. There was a roaring fire under the *paila*. Maybe she was making some sort of special potion. Maybe she was cooking cats. *¿Quién sabe?"* Tío Balde paused and took a big drink of beer. "All I know is that she took off most of her clothing and danced around that big *paila.*"

"And why were you at Señorita Sinforosa's place, anyway?" Ernesto asked and stole another drink from Tío Balde's beer.

"Because when I was coming home last night from town, I noticed that there was a full moon. So I decided to investigate the story for myself." Tío Balde stood up and stretched.

I turned toward my uncle. I couldn't keep quiet any longer. "So what happened?"

Tío Balde looked at me and slightly smiled. "Well, I slipped quietly through the bushes and hid near Señorita Sinforosa's house. And what I saw was a once in a lifetime sight!" Tío Balde threw back his head, laughed, and putting the bottle to his lips, drained the rest of the beer. "You *chamacos* should go sometime and see for yourselves, like tonight. There's a full moon."

Tío Balde had finished smoking all of his tobacco, so he asked Ernesto to go to town with him to buy some more. After they left I continued lying on the bed mulling over what our uncle had said.

"Do you believe that story about Señorita Sinforosa?" I asked Miguel.

"I really don't know. Sounds like *puro guato* to me." Miguel sucked down the small amount of beer that was left in one of the bottles. "Maybe she has a young woman visiting her and that was who Tío Balde saw."

"Are you afraid to go over to Señorita Sinforosa's place?" I asked.

"No. I'm not afraid. Are you?" Miguel reached for another of the empty bottles.

"Not at all," I answered. Of course that was a fib. I was afraid. Not afraid that Señorita Sinforosa would turn herself into a beautiful dancing girl, but afraid that she would turn herself into a cat, or a bat, or *quién sabe qué*.

"Come on. Let's go over to her place," said Miguel. Let's go before it gets too late." He jumped up from the bed and put the beer bottle down.

We quickly crossed our father's plowed field without talking. The full moon made it easy to see where we were going. I felt a little anxious when we entered the dark *monte*. Miguel led the way down the path to Señorita Sinforosa's house.

"Over there," whispered Miguel as he motioned for me to go toward an old *guallín* that was standing not too far from the house.

We hunkered down under the wagon and waited. The moon lit up Señorita Sinforosa's yard. There were two cats lying near the doorway of the house. One was licking its paws, the other was doing nothing. A black *paila* was sitting over a small fire not far from the woodpile, and a galvanized washtub sat on a fruit crate nearby. I wondered how long Miguel would expect us to wait there looking at nothing.

I had just stretched out to get more comfortable when Señorita Sinforosa came out of her house. She carried some items in her hands that she laid out on a small stool that was sitting next to the galvanized washtub. Next, she removed something from her white hair causing it to tumble down her back. She then removed her dress and shoes and stood before us in a suit of loose-fitting underwear that looked very similar to the one-piece suit that Abuelo Angel wore.

I sat up on my haunches to prepare myself for running away the instant Señorita Sinforosa turned herself into a cat. The old woman walked over to the *paila* and stuck her hand in it. I heard a splashing sound. Then Señorita Sinforosa took a small bucket and filled it with the liquid from the *paila*. She bent over the washtub and poured the liquid from the bucket over her hair. Next, she retrieved something from the stool and began rubbing it into her hair.

"Washing her hair. Just an old woman washing her hair," whispered Miguel.

I thought he sounded a little disappointed. I didn't say anything because I was concentrating on everything Señorita Sinforosa did so as not to miss the moment she turned herself into something. I really hoped it would be the almost naked dancing girl. I had never seen a naked woman or an almost naked one. The idea was titillating.

Señorita Sinforosa rinsed her hair and wrapped her head with the dress she had taken off. She picked up the washtub and proceeded to throw the water on the fire, but in doing so, she tripped and fell to the ground. I heard her cry out, then there was nothing but a sound of low moaning as she lay writhing on the ground.

Miguel jumped out from under the wagon and ran to the old woman. "Are you badly hurt, Señorita Sinforosa?" Miguel asked.

I thought he was foolish. What if it was a trick to lure us out? Maybe she knew we had been watching her and now had something terrible planned for us. I thought we should run away from there but I didn't want to be separated from Miguel, so I followed him.

"*Ay*, it's my ankle. I've skinned my ankle on that old crate," Señorita Sinforosa said.

I looked down and saw a frail-looking woman lying on the ground who was apparently in pain because she was crying.

Miguel reached down and helped her get to her feet.

"Who are you boys? Why are you here?" She stopped crying and looked carefully at us.

"We're Sigifredo Balderas's sons, and we are just looking for our dogs. Yes, that's why we're here. Our dogs are lost," said Miguel.

"So you're Sigi's boys. Well, your dogs are not here, and I haven't seen them. I'm so sorry," Señorita Sinforosa said. She attempted to walk, but she appeared a little unsteady. "Will you boys help me get into my house, please?"

Miguel took one of her arms and I took the other, and together, we helped her into her kitchen. It looked nice and clean and inviting in the glow of a kerosene lamp. There was a bowl of apples on the table and a white enamel coffeepot warming on the wood-burning range.

We put Señorita Sinforosa on one of the kitchen chairs. She took a silk shawl that was draped over the back of the chair and wrapped it around her small bony shoulders. Then she inspected her ankle, which didn't seem to be badly injured.

"It's just scraped, *gracias a Dios*," she said. "Hand me that cloth, please." She smiled and motioned for me to hand her a cloth that was hanging on a hook. Then she pointed to a shelf above the washstand. "Will you see if there is a can of Watkins salve on the shelf, please?"

I handed her the cloth and the flat can of salve, and she began to clean the scrapes on her ankle. Miguel and I stood in her kitchen and watched. I noticed that Señorita Sinforosa had a very pleasant-looking face. She had soft features and a friendly smile. She didn't look like what I had expected a witch to look like. I decided that she must not really be a witch after all.

"Do you boys want some coffee?" Señorita Sinforosa asked as she put the lid back on the salve can.

"No, thank you. We really need to go home," answered Miguel.

"Well, then, let me wrap you each an *empanada* to take home. They're made from fresh *calabaza,* and I made them only this morning." She removed a piece of muslin cloth that covered a plate of pumpkin turnovers that sat on the sideboard. She took a piece of butcher paper, wrapped two of the small delicacies, and tied the package with a piece of twine. She smiled at us and thanked us for helping her with her injured ankle.

"*Oigan, muchachos.* Please come back to visit me when you can. And bring your sisters. I do get so very lonely here by myself."

We thanked her for the *empanadas* and left her house. As we retraced our route across the plowed fields, we discussed our assessment of Señorita Sinforosa's witchhood.

"Well, what do you think?" I asked Miguel.

"About what?"

"If Señorita Sinforosa is a witch or not," I said.

"My goodness, Alejandro, did you ever really think she was?" Miguel stopped in the middle of the field and squarely faced me.

"Well, I thought she might be. And Tío Balde thinks she is. And you heard what he said about her. And I just didn't know," I stammered.

"Don't be so stupid! There aren't really any witches."

"Then why did we go to Señorita Sinforosa's?" I asked.

"We went to prove that Tío Balde was wrong." Miguel turned and began walking toward home.

Ernesto and Tío Balde were in the house when we arrived. They both smiled as Tío Balde asked, "Well, where have you two night owls been? To Señorita Sinforosa's place?" He opened a little cloth bag of tobacco and shook some out onto a small piece of paper.

"Yes. That's where we've been," said Miguel without looking at Tío Balde or Ernesto.

"Oh, how very interesting," said Tío Balde as he rolled himself a cigarette. "And did you by chance see the beautiful dancing girl?"

"Yes. We saw her and we talked to her," said Miguel.

"And she invited us into her kitchen and gave us each an *empanada*," I quickly added and held up the package that Señorita Sinforosa had given us.

Miguel turned his back to us because I think he was ready to burst out laughing.

"Let me see," said Tío Balde who was no longer smiling.

Ernesto said nothing but stared at us with a look of curiosity on his face.

I slowly unwrapped the butcher paper from around the *empanadas* and gave Miguel his. He and I proceeded to eat the delicious turnovers without offering them as much as a tiny bite.

Tío Balde lit his cigarette, took a puff, and said, "You're lying. You never went over to Señorita Sinforosa's place." "Oh, yes we did," I replied. "The beautiful dancing girl told us to come back anytime we wanted and to bring Rosa and Virginia, too." "It's true," said Miguel. "We'll probably go back tomorrow night to check on her ankle. She hurt it when she was dancing around her cauldron." Miguel licked a piece of pumpkin from his upper lip.

Tío Balde said nothing. He ran his index finger over the butcher paper that I had laid on the bed. I guess there must have been a crumb because he put his finger to his mouth. Without saying anything, he turned and walked out of our sleeping house. He never again mentioned the almost naked dancing girl.

VII

The Canal

As we boys got older, we discontinued the Saturday bath-house ritual and graduated to bathing in the cement irrigation canal or in the drainage ditch that was connected to it by a large cement pipe. It didn't take long for bathing to become a time for having great fun.

"Here, Alejandro, catch," our cousin Cándido would yell from the canal bank as he drew his arm back in a posture of pitching a ball.

Happily, I would raise my hands out of the water in anticipation. Sometimes Cándido threw a ball of some kind, but usually it was a rock or a clod of dirt. Occasionally, he threw my clothing into the water. He seemed to get enjoyment from bullying me and Miguel, but especially me.

One hot afternoon when Miguel and I were bathing in the canal, Cándido walked up to the edge of the canal and yelled at me to catch. I put out my hands. Splat. Something hit me in the face. Splat, splat. It hit again. My eyes began to burn, and the stench gagged me. I realized it was fresh cow manure, and I quickly went down under the water. I think I could hear Cándido laughing even with my ears full of manure and canal water.

"Stop that! That's not funny!" Miguel called to Cándido who was pulling off his clothing and laughing.

"Hey, *tonto*, who do you think you are?" Cándido said as he jumped into the water with us.

I had by this time cleaned the manure from my face and hair. My eyes were still burning. I saw Miguel start toward Cándido.

"I'll show you who *el tonto* is when I catch you," said Miguel. Miguel was usually not aggressive, but could on occasion rise to a level of rage that was awesome. Papá said he got this trait from Mamá's side of the family.

Cándido threw back his head and laughed loudly, and then swam toward the submerged cement pipe that connected the canal to the drainage ditch. He disappeared down under the water. I thought nothing of this. Cándido often swam through the long pipe, coming out over in the ditch where he usually taunted the rest of us for being afraid to swim through the pipe. And we were afraid. Mamá had told us never to do that because it was dangerous.

I decided to get out of the water because of my burning eyes.

"Alejandro, can you see Cándido?" Miguel asked.

I walked over to the drainage ditch and looked for Cándido. He was nowhere to be seen.

"Do you see him?" Miguel asked again.

"No. He hasn't come out," I replied.

"Hurry, go get Papá or Ernesto," Miguel said as he swam toward the pipe opening.

I ran in the direction of the compound in my wet, sagging underwear. "Papá! Papá!" I screamed.

Mamá came out of the house. "Your father is not here. What's wrong?"

"Cándido didn't come out of the pipe." I pointed toward the canal.

Mamá said nothing but ran toward the canal. Miguel had jumped into the ditch to see if Cándido was somewhere under the water.

"Mamá, I can't find Cándido. He swam into the pipe," Miguel yelled.

Mamá quickly pulled off her shoes and her long cotton stockings. Then she jumped into the canal and swam into the pipe.

I could not believe what Mamá had just done. I held my breath. Mamá did not come out. Miguel swam toward the mouth of the pipe as Mamá came up gasping for air. She held a lifeless Cándido in her arms.

Miguel helped Mamá lay Cándido out on the ground.

"There is thick brush plugging the pipe. Cándido was caught in it," Mamá said as she breathed laboriously.

We could see scratches on Cándido's body and on Mamá's arms. Cándido lay on the ground with his eyes closed. He didn't appear to be breathing.

Ernesto and several of the seasonal farmworkers were coming in from the fields. I called to them, and they quickly came over. Two of the workers held Cándido upside down by his feet and shook him. Water came out of his mouth and nose. Next they put Cándido on his stomach and pressed hard on his back. I saw water running out of his mouth. They did this until Cándido began coughing and gasping for air.

"What's happened to my boy?" Tía Inocencia came running up to the small group that had gathered around Cándido.

"He nearly drowned in the pipe. Mamá pulled him out," said Miguel.

"Are you all right, *mi'jo*? Who hurt you?" Tía Inocencia asked, running her hand over the scratches on Cándido's chest.

Cándido didn't say anything. He just sat up and began crying.

Mamá and Miguel tried to explain to Tía Inocencia what had happened, but the woman seemed so determined to blame someone that I guess she didn't understand what was being said.

Instead of thanking Mamá for going into the pipe to save her son, Tía Inocencia said, "I've told Cándido not to play with your boys, Ramona. They're so rough and rowdy. I'm afraid for my boy, and now just look at what has happened."

Cándido never seemed the same after that day. He had problems doing simple things like tying his shoes. He was kicked out of school because he would pee in his pants. Tía Inocencia reported that his teacher told her that Cándido was too old to be displaying such infantile behavior and that he would be welcomed back in class as soon as he was potty trained again. Tía Inocencia was very angry at the teacher and the school.

"My poor boy. *Está enfermito. Está enfermo de los nervios*," Tía Inocencia told everyone she knew.

"No, no, no. It's not his nerves," said Abuelo Angel.

Abuela Luciana said, "*Ay, Dios mío. Le hicieron mal de ojo*." She thought someone had put the curse of the evil eye on him.

"No one has put a curse on him," said Abuelo Angel. "Listen to me. Cándido's brain has been damaged from him being under the water too long. I've seen this happen before."

Abuela Luciana insisted on giving Cándido her special egg treatment, so she lit a candle for Our Lady of Guadalupe and laid the boy on her bed. She then took an egg and rubbed it all over Cándido's body as she recited her repertory of prayers. Finally, she broke the egg into a bowl of water and inspected it closely. Unfortunately, Cándido's condition made little improvement.

"My son needs a good *curandero*," said Tía Inocencia.

So she and Tío Erasmo took Cándido to Mexico, where they paid the best folk healers they could find to treat Cándido. When that didn't help, Cándido's parents, at Abuelo Angel's urging, took their son to a brain specialist in San Antonio. Tía Inocencia said she wasn't pleased with the reports and insisted on taking Cándido to a specialist in Houston. By that time Tío Erasmo had no money left, so they came back to Chicken Foot Farm.

Mamá told us to be kind to Cándido and help look after him, which we did. Cándido seemed to want to be with us, and he followed us all over the farm. He quit wetting his pants, and he learned to tie his shoes again. We taught him how to do chores, and in time he became a good worker.

Tío Erasmo said that because he had spent all his money getting Cándido cured, he needed to go to California for the summer. He had been told he could make a fortune in the fruit and vegetable harvests. Tía Inocencia, Cándido, and Roque went with him so they could also work to make their fortune.

VIII

La Novia

I had just arrived home from school when Toribio Tovar delivered the *esquela*. He quietly handed the black-edged note through the doorway to Mamá. She thanked him and shut the door.

"Who could it be?" she said as she unfolded the dreaded death announcement and began to read.

"Well, hurry and tell us," Virginia said and held out her hand to take the *esquela* as if not wanting to wait for Mamá to finish reading it.

"*Pobre* Señorita Sinforosa," said Mamá as she handed the *esquela* to Virginia.

"Señorita Sinforosa! How sad. I had been thinking of her only this morning," Virginia said.

I thought how foolish I was for previously thinking that the nice old woman could have been a witch. Miguel and I went back to her house after the night we hid under her wagon and watched as she washed her hair. We took our sisters to visit her just as she had requested of us, and once Abuela Luciana went along with us. I thought of how Señorita Sinforosa served us mugs of hot steamy coffee, pumpkin turnovers, and pig-shaped ginger cookies. Now she was dead. I wanted to know when and how it had happened. Tía Inocencia soon came to tell us the whole story.

"I tell you, it's a sad day when an old woman like Señorita Sinforosa has to die alone. There's no excuse for that. She has sisters and nieces. Someone should have been with her."

"Yes, you're correct, Inocencia. I think she used to live in Brownsville with one of her sisters," Mamá said and wiped her eyes with her white batiste handkerchief. "I don't know why she chose to live alone in her older years."

"Just think," Tía Inocencia continued. "Yesterday morning the Watkins salesman found poor Sinforosa dead on her kitchen floor. If he hadn't opened the door and looked in, she may have stayed there for weeks or even months."

"And if she hadn't been such a good customer of that Watkins salesman, he wouldn't have even been at her house to find her dead body," said Virginia.

I turned toward Tía Inocencia. "What killed her?"

Tía Inocencia narrowed her eyes and leaned toward me. "It was her heart. I heard that when the Watkins man found her, her face was bright purple, and that means only one thing: heart attack. And her body was already cold when he found her." Tía Inocencia shivered and fastened a wisp of her oily hair back with a bobby pin.

"Perhaps she just died of old age. She must have been more than eighty years old," said Rosa.

"She lived a long life," Mamá said. "Sinforosa and her family have known the Balderas family for many years. We'll go to the *velorio* tonight. I want my children to pay their respects."

That night our family went to the wake at Señorita Sinforosa's house. *Velorios* were not events that I preferred to attend, but Mamá said it was our duty to the dead. I really didn't want to see Señorita Sinforosa with a bright purple face but, of course, I had no choice but to do as I was told.

When we arrived at the wake there were a few neighbors in the kitchen, along with some members of Señorita Sinforosa's family. Papá, Ernesto, and Miguel stayed out in the yard with some of the men. They would pay their respects later. To one of Señorita Sinforosa's sisters, Mamá gave the pound of ground coffee and the dozen *molletes* that we had brought. The kitchen smelled of strong coffee, pig-shaped ginger cookies, and kerosene lamps. I peered into the parlor and saw a few people sitting around a coffin that was placed on a black-skirted base. Mamá motioned for us to pass on through the kitchen. Rosa and Virginia led the way into the parlor, and Mamá quietly led me up to the coffin.

I looked carefully at Señorita Sinforosa's face. It wasn't purple as I had expected. In fact, her face looked just as it always did except now maybe a little paler and certainly less animated than usual. Mamá knelt beside the coffin.

I heard Rosa giggle. She and Virginia began whispering to one another and pointing down at the dead woman. I moved closer to get a better look. There, in the wooden coffin, lay Señorita Sinforosa dressed in a white satin bridal gown. On her head was a tiara to which a long veil was attached. Her hands held a glass rosary and a bouquet of dingy white lilies made of paper.

"She's dressed like a *novia*," Virginia whispered. "What's wrong with these people?"

"They must be crazy," Rosa responded and then she giggled.

Mamá quickly arose and grabbed Rosa's arm with one hand and Virginia's arm with the other. She escorted my sisters out of the parlor and into the kitchen. I didn't know why Mamá seemed angry, and I didn't know for sure why Rosa had giggled. I suspected, however, that it had something to do with Señorita Sinforosa looking like a bride. I looked down at the dead woman one last time and rushed into the kitchen to join Mamá and my sisters.

Mamá shook her finger at Rosa and said in a low voice, "How could you embarrass me like this?"

Rosa said nothing, but smiled strangely, hunched her shoulders, and pointed at Virginia.

Mamá turned toward Virginia. "And you are absolutely too old to be acting like a silly child."

"I'm so sorry, Mamá. I was just taken by surprise when I saw Señorita Sinforosa dressed like a bride." Tears began to roll down Virginia's face.

"It's an old custom," said Mamá. "When a maiden lady dies without ever being wed, she has the right to be buried as a bride. Señorita Sinforosa most likely requested to be buried like this."

"She certainly did," responded one of Señorita Sinforosa's sisters who was sitting in the kitchen and had observed the exchange between Mamá and my sisters. "In fact, Sinforosa reminded me many times not to forget to dress her as a bride. She had the gown made several years ago and had packed it away to use for this occasion. I bought the tiara and veil for her myself."

Mamá apologized to Señorita Sinforosa's sister for the lack of decorum displayed by my sisters and then decided that it was time for us to go home. We didn't even stay for some of the coffee and sweet bread that we had brought.

Before going to bed that night, I overheard Virginia and Rosa discussing the events of the evening as they cleaned the kitchen. They talked about the bridal gown, the tiara, and the flowers.

"Those paper lilies were ugly. I think they should have used real flowers," said Virginia. She scowled and took the bowl I had just emptied from the table.

"Well, I think the entire custom is rather strange," responded Rosa. "Just think about it. A woman who is never a bride during her life becomes one in death."

"Oh, I don't think that's so terrible," said Virginia as she untied her apron.

Rosa turned from the counter that she was wiping and faced Virginia. In a somber voice she said, "Well, *hermana*, since you don't seem to be receiving any marriage proposals, I hope you don't expect me to dress your dead body in a wedding dress and put a veil and tiara on your head."

"Did I ask you to do that? I didn't hear anyone ask you to do that. Alejandro, did you hear anyone ask Rosa to do that?" Virginia was apparently angered.

I didn't say a word. I don't know how that conversation ended because I hurried out of the kitchen. I went directly to the sleeping house and went to bed. Before I fell asleep, I spent some time thinking of pumpkin turnovers, pig-shaped ginger cookies, and dead women dressed as brides.

IX

A City Cousin

It was in late August when we received a message that my grandfather Marcos Martínez was very ill. Mamá Lola, as we called my maternal grandmother, wanted Mamá to come to San Antonio as soon as possible.

"I think you should take me, Sigifredo," Mamá said. "The bus trip is long and tiring. I won't be much help to my mother if I'm exhausted when I get there."

"That's true," Papá said, and he gazed out the door toward the north. "I'll get the pickup ready."

Mamá said that I would go with them so Papá wouldn't have to drive back home alone. Ernesto had to stay to take care of the farm for Papá. Rosa, Virginia, and Miguel would be looked after by Abuelo Angel and Abuela Luciana. So it was with great enthusiasm and expectations that I squeezed into the cab of the pickup truck between Mamá and Papá to make the trip to San Antonio.

We rode quietly for many miles through ranch land for as far as we could see. My father would break the silence from time to time by whistling old Mexican tunes through his teeth. This irritated Mamá, and she usually said so. Occasionally, Papá would comment on points of interest.

As we were going through a small village he said, "Look, Alejandro. See that tree over there?"

I leaned forward and peered through the passenger side window. I saw a large, live oak tree.

"Your mother saw a man hanging from that tree when she was a little girl. Isn't that so, Ramona?"

"Yes, it's true," Mamá said. "But I don't like to think about it."

"Who hung him?" I asked.

"*Pues quién sabe* . . . Maybe the sheriff did it," Mamá answered.

"It was probably the Rangers," Papá said. He clenched his teeth because I saw the muscles on the side of his jaw tighten.

"Did you see it happen, Mamá?" I was excited to know more about the hanging.

"No, I didn't see them hang him. I was just passing through in a wagon with my parents. We were going back to San Antonio from Oakville." Mamá wiped the perspiration from her face with her blue lace handkerchief and said no more about the incident.

The day became hot, and the warm air in the cab of the truck made me sweaty and sleepy. The floorboard of the pickup felt hot from the engine, so I was relieved when we stopped for gasoline. We all got out at the filling station to have some refreshments. I drank a Delaware Punch as usual, because I liked its taste and the way it made my teeth feel as if they were crumbling when I rubbed them together. The rest of the trip to San Antonio seemed to pass quickly, probably because we talked and laughed, and Mamá sang a few songs for us.

My grandparents lived on the south side of San Antonio, so we didn't get to see much of the city before we arrived at their white clapboard house. Several cement pots planted with ferns sat on the porch that wrapped around three sides of the house.

I wanted to run my hands through those strange plants to see what they felt like, but I didn't do it. On the porch near the front door were large wooden chairs painted blue. A blue wooden swing hung by chains from the porch ceiling. This house was different than the little wooden houses that we had at Chicken Foot Farm.

On one side of my grandparents' house was the little mercantile store that Abuelo Marcos had owned since his father died many years before. My great-grandfather had originally built the little store. Tío Onécimo, one of Mamá's brothers, lived in a house on the other side of my grandparents' house. Tío Onécimo had seven sons, the youngest of which was Ubaldo who was standing on my grandparents' front porch when we arrived.

"Hey, ¿*qué tal?*" Ubaldo asked as he looked at me through the slits of his half-opened eyes.

"I'm okay. How's it going with you?" I said.

"*Así, así,*" he answered and slightly grinned.

I didn't say anything else to him, and I headed for the front door of the house.

"Hey, don't you remember me?" Ubaldo said.

Of course I remembered him. How could I forget him? The last time he came with his parents to visit us at Chicken Foot Farm, he and Cándido ganged up on me and punched me around a lot. Ubaldo was four years older than me, and I couldn't have defended myself even if Cándido hadn't been his assistant. I noticed Ubaldo hadn't changed much, he was just a little taller. He wore a fancy shirt and pleated trousers. His leather shoes were highly polished.

I ignored Ubaldo and walked into the house. My grandparents had a very large front room that served as a parlor as well as their bedroom. Abuelo Marcos was there in a big bed, seemingly asleep, and looking very sick. Mamá Lola hugged me, kissed my forehead, and said that she was glad to see me and that I looked large to be only ten. Several of Mamá's sisters were there, and I greeted each of them. They patted my cheek.

"*Tan chulo*," said Tía Pilar.

"*Tan precioso*," said Tía Jupertina as she rubbed my face.

Mamá looked at me and smiled. I felt embarrassed because I thought I was too old to be admired in such a way by my aunts. I especially didn't like them calling me cute and precious.

I walked over to the bed and looked down at Abuelo Marcos. His skin looked pale, and his once feathery white mustache and beard now appeared limp and yellowed. I thought of the tall, muscular man he used to be, friendly, busy, and always impeccably dressed in a black three-piece suit and shiny hightop leather shoes.

"Mamá, why does Abuelo Marcos dress in those funny clothes?" I had asked.

"Those aren't funny clothes. You're just accustomed to seeing farmers and ranchers. Your grandfather is a merchant, and he dresses like a businessman."

Now, as I stood looking down at Abuelo Marcos, I realized that he was gravely ill. I wondered if he would ever again be well enough to go back to his little store, a place that I had always enjoyed visiting.

Papá and some of Mamá's brothers went into the backyard to visit and drink their refreshments. They sat in wooden chairs in the shade of the live oak trees. I sat with them for a little while and then went back into the house. I entered through a small room that Mamá Lola called the service porch. This room contained the electric refrigerator, storage cupboards, a tall brass urn full of umbrellas, and the exit door to the backyard. This was where deliveries were made and the trash was taken out to be burned in an incinerator near the alley. The kitchen was next to the service porch and could be closed off from the rest of the house.

"Guests shouldn't have to smell the fish before they sit down to eat it," Mamá Lola had said when I asked her why she always cooked with the kitchen door closed.

The kitchen was dominated by a large, round oak table. An electric light fixture hung low over the table. I reached over to the wall and pushed the button that turned on the light and then pushed another button that turned it off. I pushed the buttons several times just to hear the click-clacking as the lightbulb flickered on and off. Electricity was something we didn't have at Chicken Foot Farm. This amazing house also had something else that we didn't have—running water and an indoor bathtub and toilet.

I left the kitchen and walked down a hall. A big black telephone hung on the wall. I had seen Abuelo Marcos use it. I remembered how he would remove the earpiece from its cradle and then yell the number that he wanted into the mouthpiece. He never telephoned us, of course, because we didn't have a telephone at Chicken Foot Farm. To get messages to us, Abuelo Marcos had to call a man he knew who had a telephone. The man lived in a town near our farm and would eventually get someone to deliver the message to us. In emergencies people usually sent telegrams that were delivered to the homes of the recipients.

"What are you doing, *primo*? Looking for something to steal?"

I was startled by Ubaldo's voice. I turned to see him looking at me with half-closed eyes and a sneer on his face.

"No. I don't steal," I answered.

"Good. Neither do I." He hesitated just a moment as he looked me up and down. "You want to go into town with me to ride the escalator?" Ubaldo said, this time with his eyes fully open and a smile on his face.

"I don't know about riding an escalator. I don't have any money. How much do the rides cost?" I said.

"Nothing, *sonso*. The escalator is free. It's just a moving staircase at a department store." Ubaldo removed a comb from his back pocket and combed back his oily black hair.

I didn't know what an escalator was and I felt a little stupid, but I decided I wanted to go with Ubaldo to find out about escalators.

Tío Onécimo drove us into the center of town and left us at a small plaza.

"That's the Alamo over there," Ubaldo pointed. "I bet you haven't studied about the Alamo in your little country school down there in the Valley."

"Of course we've learned about the Alamo, and Davy Crockett and Jim Bowie and the others. What do you think we are?"

Ubaldo ignored my question and motioned for me to follow him down the street. We entered a beautiful building that I thought might be a hotel, but I wasn't sure.

"Just look at this place," Ubaldo said. "Look at those fancy lights and the nice furniture. I bet you don't have anything like this down there in the Valley."

Before I could even respond, an angry-looking man in a gray suit quickly walked up to us. "What business do you boys have in here?"

"We're just looking," answered Ubaldo.

"Well, get out of here immediately, or I'll call the police," the man said and pointed toward the door where we had come in.

We quickly removed ourselves from the premises and headed for the place where we could ride the escalator. We arrived at a large department store where no one confronted us when we entered. Ubaldo led the way to the escalator, and he jumped on and started moving upward. I stopped and watched him as he looked back over his shoulder and laughed. I had never seen such a thing. Of course I had seen stairways because we had those in my school building. But to see moving stairs on which you ride was a little intimidating. It was especially frightening for me to see the place where the noisy stairs were coming out from under the floor. I just couldn't get on that thing.

Ubaldo was almost up to the top when he yelled, "Come on *primo*, jump on."

I stood my ground. Others were going around me and getting on the moving stairs. Then Ubaldo did something that defied belief. He ran back down the escalator although the stairs were going up.

He grasped my upper arm and began pulling me toward the escalator. "Come on, *primo*. Stop acting like a girl. Be a man. Get on this thing."

Before I knew what had happened, I was on the escalator holding on to Ubaldo's arm with both of my hands. I looked down at my shoes, hoping they would not disappear down under the moving stairs. As we approached the top, Ubaldo pulled away from me and hopped off the stairs just before they disappeared into the floor. I had no choice but to get off somehow, so I vaulted off as high as I could possibly leap. We spent the next half hour going up and down the escalators.

Ubaldo decided we needed to return to the little plaza so we wouldn't miss Tío Onécimo when he came to pick us up. When we arrived at the plaza my uncle was nowhere in sight. I sat down on a bench to watch a flock of pigeons that were pecking around on the ground nearby. Ubaldo saw several of his friends standing across the street from the plaza. He told me to wait for him, and he went to talk to his friends. As I sat and reflected on the escalator adventure, a loud sharp meowing interrupted my thoughts. It seemed to be coming from the area of a bench across from me where a raggedy-looking man was sitting.

"Stop your crying, *gatito*," the man said as he extracted a small gray kitten from inside a soiled burlap bag.

The animal continued its loud cries although the man held the kitten and talked softly to it. Finally, he put the kitten down on the ground. It proceeded to follow after almost everyone that walked past. Several times the raggedy man arose from the bench and retrieved the kitten.

"Here you go, *gatito*," the man said as he placed a piece of what appeared to be *pan dulce* on the ground in front of the kitten.

The kitten put his nose to the food but didn't eat. I couldn't believe that an adult could be so foolish. The poor kitten really needed his mother's milk but he was being offered sweet bread instead. When the kitten didn't eat, the man put it in the burlap bag and walked away. I was glad not to have to watch the starving animal any longer.

The pigeons flocked around the remnants of the sweet bread. I noticed one pigeon seemed injured or sick and had huddled down under a bench. A man sitting nearby spotted the pigeon and went to it and picked it up. He took it to a woman who was holding a young child. The man rubbed the pigeon's tail feathers on the child's face. The child cried out and tried to pull away. The woman continued to hold on to the child and made no effort to avoid what was happening.

I was relieved that Tío Onécimo arrived at that moment to take Ubaldo and me back to my grandparents' house. I related the events that I had witnessed concerning the kitten and the pigeon to Tío Onécimo and Ubaldo.

They shrugged their shoulders and said nothing more than, "Oh."

Early the next morning Papá and I said good-bye to Mamá and her family and left San Antonio to return to Chicken Foot Farm. For many miles Papá and I discussed escalators, kittens, pigeons, and cousins.

"I'm glad that I came to San Antonio with you, Papá, but I'm happier to be going back home."

"That's good to know, *mi'jo*." Papá smiled and began whistling an old Mexican song.

We had been home only three days when Papá received a telegram from Mamá telling us that Abuelo Marcos had died. That was a sad time, especially for Mamá. Three months later Mamá Lola died.

"Mamá Lola wasn't even sick," I told Abuela Luciana. "Abuelo Marcos was too sick to live, and I can understand that. But why did Mamá Lola have to die?"

Abuela Luciana raised her left eyebrow. "I think I know why," she said. "Sometimes when married people have been together for many, many years, the one that is left behind just doesn't want to go on living, and they die too so they can join their partner." Abuela Luciana patted my arm and handed me a large spoon.

"If Abuelo Angel dies, are you going to die too?" I asked.

Abuela Luciana pushed the peanut butter toward me and smiled. "Absolutely not. In fact, I might just live forever."

X

The Conflagration

"You can't be hungry. You had two big bowls of *avena* for breakfast and three *tacos de barbacoa* for lunch." Abuela Luciana, who was alone in the kitchen, looked at me and shook her head.

"But, I really am hungry," I said trying to appear famished. Abuela was correct about what I had eaten. But I was hungry, so I had come to the kitchen.

"Here. You can have one of these." Abuela Luciana turned from the stove and handed me a warm tortilla.

"*Gracias,*" I said and walked to the doorway eating the tortilla. I looked out across the family compound. It was a quiet Sunday afternoon in early December. The South Texas sun was shining with a brilliance that made the mesquite trees shimmer and seem to dance.

"Wait, Alejandro." Abuela Luciana motioned for me to come back and sit down at the long wooden table where she had placed a small bowl of *fideo*. She turned and began adding wood to the stove. I watched her through half-closed eyes as I slowly ate the tasty pasta.

My moment of delight was rudely interrupted when our neighbor, Toribio Tovar, came running through the compound yelling for Abuelo Angel.

"Don Angel, Don Angel! Have you heard? We've been attacked!" Toribio burst through the entrance of the kitchen, panting from running no farther than from his pickup that he had parked in front of our house.

"Doña Luciana! Where is Don Angel? Where is Sigifredo?"

Abuela Luciana turned toward Toribio with an apparent look of distress on her face. "*Ay, Dios mío*. They've gone to get firewood. What's wrong with you?"

"Haven't you heard? The United States Navy has been attacked," Toribio said as he gasped for air.

"Are you sure? How do you know this?" Abuela Luciana said and steadied herself by holding on to the table's edge.

"*De veras*, Doña Luciana. I swear it's true. I heard it from Gabriel Moreno who heard it on the radio at his brother's house in town."

"Well, sit a while and catch your breath." Abuela Luciana turned toward the stove and poured Toribio a cup of steaming coffee from the large blue enameled pot.

"It's all so terrible," said Toribio as he reached to take the coffee cup from Abuela Luciana's hand. He still appeared somewhat out of breath, and I noticed that his hands trembled as he added four teaspoons of sugar to his coffee.

By the time Toribio had drunk three cups of coffee and I had eaten another tortilla, Papá and Abuelo Angel had arrived. Papá brought in an armful of mesquite wood and put it down by the stove. Abuelo Angel greeted Toribio and sat down beside me at the table.

Papá joined us and looked at Toribio. "Is something wrong?"

Toribio took a big breath and quickly said that the United States Navy had been attacked.

"What do you mean attacked? How was the Navy attacked?" Abuelo Angel asked.

"I'm not sure. I think airplanes dropped bombs on the ships." Toribio was now on his fourth cup of coffee. He wiped the perspiration from his face with his faded red bandana. He was still shaken.

"Who did it?" asked Papá.

"Some kind of Orientals. I think maybe Japanese." Toribio handed his empty cup to Abuela Luciana.

Abuela Luciana refilled Toribio's cup and poured cups for Papá and Abuelo Angel. "*Ay, Dios mío.* Where did this happen, Toribio? Surely you must know that."

"Yes, Doña Luciana, I do know. It happened in the Hawaiian Islands."

"Are we in any danger? Will they bomb us, too?" Abuela Luciana turned toward Abuelo.

Abuelo Angel did not immediately respond, but when he did his demeanor was assuring. "No, they have no reason to bomb us. We aren't near Japan or the Hawaiian Islands."

I stopped eating and listened carefully to the adults. This thing that had happened was very upsetting to them. I knew where the Hawaiian Islands were, and also Japan. At least I knew where they were on the world map that hung on the wall in my sixth-grade classroom. That was all they were to me, places on a map.

Mamá and other family members began to gather in the kitchen. Toribio repeated his story several times. Someone suggested that Tío Balde set up his battery-operated radio in the kitchen so that we could hear the news reports.

All afternoon, members of the family sat around the radio that was placed in the middle of the long wooden table. We listened to accounts that told of the unexpected attack by the Japanese planes that had brought horrible destruction to our ships and death to many people. As I and my family listened to the reports concerning the attack at Pearl Harbor, I sensed that something terrible might happen to us, not only as a nation but as a family. I saw Mamá shiver several times as she sat on the long bench next to Papá.

"Sigi, are you sure we aren't in any danger? What does this mean? Are we in a war?" Mamá sought answers and assurances from Papá.

"We aren't in a war yet, but I'm afraid that this attack on our Navy will lead to war." Papá stood up, stretched, and then sat down again on the bench.

"Will Balde and Ernesto have to go to the Army?" Mamá asked. She waved a fly away from the edge of the sugar bowl.

"I'll go," said Ernesto. He had been sitting quietly at the table, apparently listening intently to the radio broadcast. "I want to go!"

Papá spoke quickly. "No, Ernesto! I need you here on the farm. You don't need to go to the Army."

Abuela Luciana began blessing Ernesto by repeatedly making the sign of the cross as she whispered, "*Dios te bendiga, hijo.*"

Trying to sound very serious, I said, "I'll join the Army if the United States goes to war." I looked over at Miguel who frowned at me but said nothing.

Abuela Luciana gasped. "*Ay, madre de Dios.*"

Papá looked up. "You're only eleven years old, Alejandro. You can't join the Army." He pulled a match from his shirt pocket and lit the kerosene lamp that sat in the middle of the table. "Even if we do go to war, it can't last very long. We can whip those Japanese in no time."

Mamá smiled at Papá and wiped her eyes with her apron hem. "How do you know that?"

"Because Japan is just a bunch of little islands, not even much of a country, and certainly not a powerful nation like the United States," Papá said.

"All of this makes me afraid," said Mamá. She moved closer to Papá.

"No, the Japanese aren't to be feared," continued Papá. "It's Hitler and the Nazis that we should be watching out for." Abuelo Angel shook his head slowly and pulled at one side of his moustache. "You may be gravely mistaken about the Japanese."

Tío Erasmo and his family, who were home for the winter, had joined us in the kitchen. "We knew some Japanese while we were out in California. They seemed to be very kind and courteous people," said Tío Erasmo.

Tía Inocencia shook her finger at Tío Erasmo. "See there, Erasmo, I told you those people couldn't be trusted. Now look what they've done."

I spent most of the afternoon in the kitchen listening to the radio and observing family members as they interacted and discussed the events that had happened far away at the place called Pearl Harbor. We ate our evening meal while listening to the news reports coming over the radio. None of us said much. I think we were frightened by the uncertainty of what might happen to us.

Long after the meal was over and the kitchen was cleaned, various family members remained around the table listening to the radio.

No one spoke for a long time until finally Mamá looked at Miguel and me. "You boys need to go to bed. It's been a long day, and you have school tomorrow."

"Don't you think that school will be dismissed because of the Japanese attack?" I said.

"I'm sure school will go on as usual." Mamá looked at us sternly and then at Papá.

"Go to bed," Papá said. He covered his mouth with his hand so we wouldn't see that he was laughing at us.

Miguel and I lay awake for a while talking about the attack at Pearl Harbor. Miguel was saying something about bombs and airplanes when I drifted off to sleep. Sometime during the night I was awakened by shouts coming from the kitchen area. I arose to see the structure that housed our kitchen bathed in a roaring fire. Ernesto, Papá, and Abuelo Angel were already throwing water on the flames.

"Miguel, Alejandro! Get buckets and get up on the cistern!" Papá called to us.

We gathered all the buckets from the bathhouse and soon were filling them. Papá and Abuelo Angel grabbed the water-filled buckets from us. Cándido climbed up on the cistern to help us, but Tía Inocencia pulled him down as he loudly protested. I heard Roque crying, Abuela Luciana praying, and Mamá yelling at Papá to be careful. The dogs were barking and running around the perimeter of the burning building. Mamá's favorite rooster began crowing. Soon the entire family was busy attempting to stop the flames from devouring what was left of our kitchen. It was too late. The walls, the palm frond roof, the table and benches, all had been destroyed. Even Tío Balde's radio lay in ruin somewhere in the ugly miasma of smoke and ashes that had been our kitchen. Abuela Luciana's large cook stove stood above the smoking embers, the lone survivor of the blaze.

"The lumber was old and dry. I wonder what set it off," said Abuelo Angel. He pulled out his bandana and blew soot from his nose.

"Probably a spark from the stovepipe set fire to the fronds on the roof," said Papá who stood with slumped shoulders under the fresno tree trying to catch his breath.

"*Ay, madre de Dios*," said Abuela Luciana. She was standing apart from the family, hugging herself, and staring at the smoking debris.

For a while we all stood in silence, viewing what had been our family meeting place. Although simple and primitive, this structure was where we came together to commune, to interact, to celebrate. It was within the kitchen that the family established its unity and solidarity, and without it, I felt that we had lost something that helped make us a family.

"What will we do now?" Mamá asked.

Papá put his arm around Mamá's shoulders. "We'll build it again, a better one this time."

The United States entered the war against Japan and the European Axis powers a few days before Papá and Abuelo Angel began building a new kitchen on the spot where the old one had stood. Against Papá's wishes, Ernesto joined the Army and was soon sent overseas. He didn't get to see the finished kitchen before he left. We all missed Ernesto, but I think Papá missed him the most. We received letters from Ernesto, and I wrote some to him. I wanted to know if he had killed any Germans, but he never wrote to us about that.

The war caused us little inconvenience outside of Papá not having Ernesto to help on the farm. Tío Balde attempted to enlist in the Army but failed one of the tests. Mamá said it was because he drank beer all the time. He continued to help Papá with the farmwork. Miguel and I helped as much as we could after school.

A lot of the young men from neighboring farms went to the war. Some of the older boys quit school and joined the military. As time went by, the war became more and more a part of our lives. By summer, sugar, butter, coffee, shoes, and even gasoline and tires were becoming scarce. To buy rationed items, we received books of coupons issued by the government. Being a farmer, Papá was able to get ample gasoline for his pickup and Abuelo Angel's old farm truck. Miguel and I were no longer able to get bubble gum and Hershey candy bars. Mamá said those weren't good for us anyway.

When Mamá received our first ration books, she laughed and said, "Well, things have always been in short supply for us because of lack of money, not a war. Don't worry. We'll get by."

By collecting paper, scrap metal, and tin cans to be recycled, Rosa, Miguel, and I participated in what was referred to as the homefront effort. On Mondays, Papá gave us nickels and dimes to buy special stamps at school. We pasted the stamps into booklets, and when they were filled, they were exchanged for savings bonds. We called them war bonds because the money was used to finance the war.

Often Abuelo Angel gave us money to buy additional stamps. "You *chamacos* better not lose that money. You buy stamps for your war bonds. We don't want Ernesto running out of bullets."

Miguel and I learned to hate the three most heinous men in the world, Benito Mussolini, Hideki Tojo, and Adolf Hitler. We especially despised Hitler and saw his pictures and caricatures in many places. I'm sure I would have recognized him if I had ever seen him in person. And I'm sure I would have run away from him as fast as possible.

One day in late summer, I came into the kitchen hoping to get a wad of peanut butter to let melt in my mouth. I noticed something new in the kitchen. Someone had framed a picture of the U.S. flag and had hung it on the wall at the end of the long wooden table.

"Who hung that up there?" I asked Abuela Luciana.

"I did it," she said, never taking her eyes from the *masa* she was preparing for tortillas. "And don't ask for anything to eat. Our supper is almost ready."

I spied the jar of peanut butter sitting on the sideboard. "Why'd you hang it there?" I pointed up at the framed picture of the flag.

"It's something I can do for the war." She punched the ball of *masa* with her fist.

I backed up to the sideboard groping behind me for the peanut butter. "And what is it you can do?" I asked as I tried to open the jar behind my back.

"I can remind people that we are Americans." She hesitated and raised her left eyebrow. "Do you want me to open that peanut butter for you?"

XI

Love Letters

Virginia stood in the doorway in her best dress. "Mamá, may I go to the movies this afternoon with Pedro Ramos? He wants to pick me up here at the house."

"I'm sorry, but I can't give you permission. You need to speak to your father about that," said Mamá, who was sitting in the horsehair chair making lace. She stopped her shuttle and smiled at Virginia.

I chuckled to myself and continued hanging Mamá's new picture of the Sacred Heart of Jesus on the wall. I didn't understand why Virginia was asking permission to go to the movies with Pedro. She met him almost every Sunday afternoon in town. Often Virginia, along with Rosa, Miguel, and me, would go to the Sunday matinee. We three younger ones would sit down in front while Virginia joined Pedro in the back row. Virginia and Pedro had been doing this since their senior year in high school. Everyone who Virginia knew, except of course Papá, must have suspected that she and Pedro were sweethearts.

After I finished hanging the picture, I went out to the kitchen to find myself something to eat. Virginia was already there standing across the table from where Papá was seated.

"Please, Papá. Why can't Pedro pick me up here?"

"It's just not proper. What will people think?" Papá continued counting the pennies from the big glass jar that usually sat on his chest of drawers. "And, you have no business going out with Pedro Ramos."

"I bet if Gordon Fisher came by and asked to take me to the movies, you'd let me go," Virginia said.

Gordon was Madama Fisher's tall blonde-headed grandson who managed the Fisher farm. I had noticed that he seemed to stop by our place often, usually to discuss something with Papá. He seldom seemed to turn down a meal or even a cup of coffee, especially if Virginia was in the kitchen.

Virginia placed the palms of her hands on the table and leaned across toward Papá. Her face appeared flushed. "You'd probably force me to go to the movies with Gordon."

Virginia's seemingly bold attitude surprised me. This was something new for her. I watched as Papá looked up and cleared his throat.

"*Pues, ¿quién sabe?* I'm not sure if I'd even let you go with Gordon." Papá counted some more of the pennies and put them in stacks. "You know it's different with the Fishers; they've been our friends since I was young." Papá poured more pennies from the jar onto the table. "I think Madama's grandson is a very good man."

Virginia stood erect, clenched her fists, and quickly left the kitchen. I reached into the large earthen bowl where the tortillas were kept in hopes of finding something other than the *toallita* in which they were usually wrapped. There was one hard tortilla.

Abuela Luciana, who had been quietly tending to something on the stove, turned and touched Papá on the shoulder and said, "*Hijo*, you seem to have forgotten that Virginia is a young woman, *no es una niña*." She handed me the peanut butter and a large spoon.

"I know she's not a little girl. But as long as she lives in my house she will do as I say. That's just the way it is."

I'm sure that Virginia met Pedro at the movies that afternoon. I didn't realize that it would be their last Sunday together. That evening I heard Virginia telling Rosa that Pedro had been drafted and would be leaving for the Army on Monday.

Pedro's absence didn't end my sister's relationship with him. He bombarded her with letters that she kept hidden. She sent him lots of letters, too. Virginia, who had never seemed eager to make the quarter-mile walk down the paved road to retrieve our mail from the rural-route mailbox, now went every day. Often on Saturday mornings, I saw Gordon Fisher's green pickup truck slowly traveling alongside Virginia as she walked down the road. Virginia told Rosa that Gordon often tried to get her to ride with him down to the mailbox, but she had never accepted his invitation.

Gordon was a pest when our family attended fiestas and *bailes*. He usually spent the evening staring at Virginia or trying to get her to dance with him. During the Christmas season we saw him at most of the events that we attended. At one of the *pastorelas,* I heard Rosa ask Gordon if he was a Catholic.

"No," he said, "but I'll become one if I need to."

Rosa told Virginia what Gordon had said. "Just think, Gordon is willing to become a Catholic just to marry you."

Virginia seemed to become angry and told Rosa, "Don't you ever speak to Gordon about me, about marriage, or about becoming a Catholic!"

"*Cálmate, hermana*, I'm just trying to help you," said Rosa.

"Did I ask you to help me? Did anyone hear me ask you for help?" Virginia looked at me.

I was the only other person witnessing the interaction, so I meekly said, "No," and shrugged my shoulders.

"God knows that I have never encouraged Gordon Fisher," Virginia said.

I agreed with her, because at the dances Virginia usually refused to dance with him and tried to make me dance with her whenever she saw Gordon approaching. I wouldn't dance because I didn't know how and I didn't want to learn. The reason I went to the dances was to fraternize with my buddies and to tease some of the pretty girls. The food was usually good, too. Miguel refused to go to the dances and preferred to stay home and read books.

"Virginia, you're being rude to Gordon," Mamá said one night when we were at a wedding celebration. "*Oyes, mi'ja*, it won't hurt you to dance with him occasionally."

"*Por favor*, Mamá, he's too *chocante*. He's always bothering me, and he's asked if I want to marry him."

Mamá's face took on a surprised expression, and I moved closer so I could hear a little better, but Mamá didn't say anything.

I couldn't stand the suspense, so I asked Virginia, "Well, what did you say to him?"

Mamá hissed at me. I quickly sat down and drew my shoulders up around my head.

Virginia frowned and said, "Of course, I told him 'no.' I don't want to marry him."

Mamá said nothing, but I know she told Papá because I heard him discussing it with Abuelo Angel the next day. Papá interrupted me and my grandfather near the kitchen entrance where we were removing the kernels from dried ears of corn so that Abuela Luciana and Mamá could prepare the *nixtamal* for *tamales*. Papá and Abuelo Angel walked over to the back of our house. I continued operating the noisy *desgranadora*, but I heard enough of the conversation to understand that Papá was very pleased that Gordon wanted to marry Virginia. After all, he was from one of the wealthiest farm families in the area.

I saw Abuelo Angel shake his head. *"Cuidado, hijo,* don't force your daughter to do something she doesn't want to do." Virginia continued her daily walks to our mailbox even though the days were getting chilly. Before school had dismissed for the Christmas holidays, I had suggested to Virginia that the mail could stay in the box until Miguel, Rosa, and I arrived home from school. We could easily bring the mail home because the school bus let us out on the paved road near the box. Virginia insisted that it was not a problem for her to walk to the mailbox, and so she continued.

Many of the letters that Virginia brought home from the mailbox were from Ernesto. Virginia or Mamá usually read the letters aloud at the table after our evening meal. Occasionally, Papá would ask for Ernesto's letter to be read a second and even sometimes a third time. When Virginia received a letter from Pedro, she stayed out in the privy all afternoon reading it over and over. At least that's what Mamá told Abuela Luciana, and Rosa overheard it. Rosa, being the *chismosa* in the family, told Miguel and me everything about Virginia's business. I think everyone in the family knew about Virginia's correspondence with Pedro except Papá.

One cold and rainy morning, Papá went in his pickup truck to get our mail. I guess he thought he was saving Virginia an unpleasant walk in the rain, or perhaps he was anxious to see if there was a letter from Ernesto. When Rosa, Miguel, and I got home from school we found a rather perturbed Virginia outside. She told Rosa that she hadn't seen the day's mail, and she didn't know if Papá had picked up a letter from Pedro. We soon found out.

Toward the end of our evening meal, Papá took out a letter from his shirt pocket. I thought it was from Ernesto because it looked similar to the letters that we received from him. "Do you want to read this to us?" Papá handed the letter to Virginia. She took the letter and looked at it. "No. This letter is addressed to me. It's personal." Virginia spoke in a trembling voice.

Mamá looked up and asked, "Is it a letter from Ernesto?"

"No, it's from a Private Pedro Ramos," Papá said without looking away from Virginia. "How many letters has he written to you, Virginia?"

"Forty-three, Papá." She stuffed the letter into the front of her blouse and ran sobbing from the kitchen.

I'm not sure what actually happened later that night, but I heard from Rosa that Papá forced Virginia to write a letter to Private Pedro Ramos telling him not to write to her anymore. Papá supposedly mailed the letter himself. Virginia never again walked to the mailbox.

XII

One Gold Star

"Mamá, is something wrong?" Miguel, Rosa, and I had just arrived home from school and found Mamá sitting motionless in the horsehair chair. What looked like a document of some kind lay in her lap.

When she didn't respond, I walked over to her. "Please tell me what's wrong, Mamá." I reached for the document, but she took it and pulled it to her breast.

With her other hand she slowly wiped away a tear. "I was here alone when the two soldiers came to tell us. I'm afraid to tell your father."

I knew then that something terrible must have happened. As Mamá doubled over in deep sobs, Rosa took the document from her hand, silently read it, and handed it to me. I read the message several times before I fully understood that it said that Ernesto had been killed in the fighting somewhere in Europe.

We quickly gathered our family together in the kitchen, where Miguel read the document aloud. Each of us held the piece of paper a number of times, reading it or staring at it. I think we had problems believing that this had really happened to Ernesto. For a while, we sat in silence at the long kitchen table, each of us in our usual place. Ernesto's place now seemed more sadly vacant than it ever had since he had left for the war.

It was Papá who finally said, "I want Ernesto's body sent home. I won't believe my son is dead until I see his body." He hit his fist on the table.

"Maybe it's all a mistake. Maybe he's really not dead," Mamá said.

"Will they send his body home?" Miguel asked.

Papá looked down at the table and slowly shook his head. "Who knows what will be done."

"They have to send him home. How can we have a funeral for him if his body isn't here?" Virginia covered her face with her hands and sobbed.

Abuelo Angel reached across the table and touched Virginia's arm. "Don't think about that yet. I'm sure the government will be giving us more information."

"I just want this horrible war to be over." Virginia arose and walked away from the table.

Abuela Luciana and my sisters prepared an evening meal, but none of us had much appetite. Most of us sat at the table talking in low voices. Tío Balde was the first to leave the kitchen. He said he was going into town. He should have said he was going to the *cantina*. Mamá wept intermittently, and Abuela Luciana whispered prayers and blessed all of us numerous times. Papá said that he would go into town the next day and send a telegram to Tío Erasmo who had taken Tía Inocencia to Laredo to visit with her family. Papá said that he would also send a telegram to Tío Onécimo so that Mamá's family would know the sad news.

As the days went by Mamá and Papá busied themselves more than usual. Perhaps work made the idea of Ernesto's death a little less painful for them. I noticed that Papá stayed alone in the equipment shed a lot of the time. When I mentioned to Abuelo Angel how much sadness I felt about Ernesto, he said nothing but gave me a pat on the back and a quick hug. I wanted to talk to Tío Balde about Ernesto, but he now seemed to stay in town a lot. He wasn't helping my father with the farmwork as much as he should have.

"There's just nothing here for me anymore," Tío Balde said one night when he had come into our sleeping house to smoke cigarettes and drink beer. "I think I'm going to go down to Brownsville to look for a job." He left the next day.

Doing chores helped me to deal with some of the sadness I was feeling. When I wasn't doing work for Papá, I kept the yard clean and attended to Mamá's flower beds in front of our house. I was weeding the beds one Saturday afternoon when a big blue Lincoln sedan stopped in front of our house. The driver, a well-dressed woman with red fox tails hanging from her shoulders, got out of the driver's side and waved at me.

"Tell your Mamá we're here."

Another woman emerged from the passenger side, and the two walked past me.

Before I could get up from my knees, Mamá came running out of our house, holding her arms open to the two women approaching her.

Mamá embraced both women at the same time. "*Gracias a Dios*, you've come."

As the three women stood in our yard hugging and weeping, I suddenly recognized Mamá's sisters, Tía Pilar and Tía Jupertina. It had been before the war since we had last seen them. Both had married Navy officers and had moved to Corpus Christi where their husbands were stationed.

"*Ay, hermana*, we would have come as soon as we heard about Ernesto, but the gas rationing keeps me from doing as much traveling as I'd like." Tía Pilar pointed to her large four-door automobile and frowned.

"We're so sorry about Ernesto," said Tía Jupertina. "In his memory, we have brought you something special." She pointed to a small package that Tía Pilar had in her hand.

"Let's go to the kitchen where we can visit and have some refreshments," Mamá said as she led the two women in the direction of the kitchen.

I followed because I wanted refreshments also, maybe a drink of *tamarindo* or *jamaica*. I thought of the bag of pig-shaped ginger cookies that Abuelo Angel had brought home from the bakery only that morning.

Mamá had Tía Pilar and Tía Jupertina sit down at the kitchen table while Abuela Luciana poured them coffee from the blue enamel coffeepot that usually sat warming on the cookstove. Mamá arranged four ginger pig cookies on a white porcelain plate and placed it on the table. Then she searched through a box on the sideboard until she found the linen napkins that we never used.

"As Jupertina already said, we're so sorry about Ernesto." Tía Pilar took a ginger pig and daintily dunked it in her coffee. "We have a friend in Corpus Christi who has lost a son in the war also. She belongs to a special group of mothers."

"That's how we found out about the banners," said Tía Jupertina.

Tía Pilar quickly opened the package and laid a small white banner with a red border on the table. In the middle of the banner was one gold star.

"See, Ramona, it's a service flag, and the gold star represents Ernesto." Tía Pilar ran her index finger over the star. "Usually the stars are blue, but when the star is gold, it means that this home has lost one of its family members in the war."

Mamá said nothing but slightly smiled and nodded.

"We enrolled you in the group of mothers who have lost sons in the war," Tía Pilar said as she picked up her coffee cup with one hand and her cookie with the other. "I hope you can come occasionally to the meetings. Anyway, it will be good for you to come to Corpus Christi to visit us." Tía Pilar stuffed the remainder of her ginger pig into her mouth.

"*Pues*, I don't know." Mama sighed. "Sigifredo stays so busy. And then the tires on the pickup aren't very good." Mamá wiped her eyes with her pink handkerchief edged with white lace.

"Well, we'll just have to see about it later," Tía Jupertina said and quickly finished her coffee and wiped her mouth with the linen napkin, leaving smudges of bright red lipstick. "Let's go put the banner in your parlor window so we can see how it looks."

My aunts rushed Mamá back into the house. Abuela Luciana motioned for me to follow her to our house. We found my aunts and Mamá admiring the banner that had just been hung in our parlor window.

"Now everyone who comes to your house will see the gold star and know that you have lost your son in the war," said Tía Pilar as she adjusted the banner.

Mamá smiled and said, "Thank you for thinking of Ernesto." As Mamá stood looking at the banner, Papá stepped into the room.

Papá removed his straw hat and quickly shook hands with my aunts. "What did you say that the little flag is for?" Papá pointed toward the window.

"It's a service banner. The gold star represents Ernesto," said Tía Jupertina, and she quickly looked over to Tía Pilar who stood erect with her chin held high.

"What does that mean?" said Papá as he moved closer to the window.

"Well, it means that Ernesto has been killed in the war," said Tía Pilar.

Papá frowned. "I don't need anything hanging in my window to tell me what the government has already told me." Papá's face turned red, and he walked to the window and removed the banner.

Mamá covered her mouth with her handkerchief, closed her eyes, and bowed her head. Tía Pilar raised her chin higher and began putting on her leather gloves. Tía Jupertina quickly opened the front door and stood teetering on the threshold.

Papá's face turned redder, and he held the banner up to Tía Pilar. "Perhaps it's all a terrible mistake. I haven't seen his dead body!" Papá rolled up the banner and shook it in the face of my undaunted aunt. "I don't want to look at this banner every day, and I will not have it in my house!" He turned and walked out the back door with the banner still in his hand.

Abuela Luciana and I were watching as Papá walked directly to the garbage barrel and tossed the banner in. I don't think Mamá or my aunts saw him do that because Tía Jupertina and Tía Pilar had already walked out the front door with Mamá following them, begging them not to leave. They left anyway, and Mamá went into her room, shut the door, and cried loud enough that Abuelo Angel said later that he could hear her all the way over to his house.

After witnessing what Papá had done, Abuela Luciana said, "Well, I'll just have to take care of this." She walked out to the garbage barrel and retrieved the banner. "Come with me to my house, Alejandro. Help me hang this banner in my window." Abuela Luciana made a fist and shook it in the air. "Let's just see if your father will have *el valor* to remove Ernesto's banner from my window."

I helped Abuela Luciana hang the banner in her window. It hung there a long time. My father never attempted to remove it. It took the hand of God on a frightening and unforgettable night to remove the little banner with one gold star.

XIII

The Javalina

"What were you doing under the bed?" Miguel closed the book he was reading and looked at me.

"I was trying to find my good shoes." I held up one of my brown leather loafers.

It was Sunday, and Miguel and I were enjoying a leisurely afternoon in our sleeping house. Miguel was lying across the bed engrossed in a book as usual. I was in need of something to do, and it certainly was not reading a book. I decided to polish my leather shoes but had found only one. Again, I reached under the bed and this time I felt Ernesto's 22 caliber rifle.

"Hey, look what I found." I pulled it out and began removing the soft cloth that Ernesto had tied around it for protection.

Miguel glanced over at me and frowned. "You'd better put that back under the bed."

I ignored him. I hadn't thought of the rifle since Ernesto had left for the Army. It was a bolt-action, single-shot rifle that Mr. Fisher had given to Papá years before, and Papá had given it to Ernesto.

"Put it back, Alejandro, before you shoot yourself or somebody's pickup truck."

I knew what he meant about shooting pickup trucks. "Don't worry, I'll be careful." I opened the bottom drawer of our chifforobe where I knew there were several boxes of bullets for the rifle. I took a handful and put them in my pocket.

Miguel continued reading, so I said nothing as I walked out of the sleeping house and started toward the irrigation canal. It was disappointing to me that Miguel never seemed very interested in doing things with me. He read a lot, and Mamá said that that was why he made good grades in high school. I was an average student in general. There were times when I almost flunked some classes, but I always made straight A's in my agriculture class. Miguel spent a lot of his time studying and doing homework. I think he used that as an excuse to get out of working on the farm.

I was excited to have Ernesto's rifle in my hands. Maybe I could kill a few rabbits. I had never killed an animal with the rifle, but I knew how to use it because Ernesto had taught me. We had set up targets on the high bank of the irrigation canal.

"Be sure you don't aim too high," Ernesto had said as he helped me hold the rifle in the correct position. "We don't want to hit Toribio's house."

I looked beyond the canal and could see Toribio Tovar's house about a half mile away. "The bullets won't go that far, will they?"

Ernesto laughed and shrugged his shoulders. "I'm not sure, but we don't want to take a chance."

We spent about an hour that day shooting at cans that we had placed along the canal bank. I was very careful to aim low so I wasn't prepared for what happened later that day when Toribio Tovar came to show Papá the bullet hole in the roof of his Studebaker pickup truck.

"Don't try to tell me your boys weren't out shooting today, Sigifredo. I know the bullet came from your direction." Toribio stood beside his pickup and pointed. "Just take a look at the hole the bullet made."

"Rather large hole," Papá said, "especially for a 22 caliber."
Papá stuck his head into the cab of the truck. "It seems the bullet was going out of your truck, not coming in. Look at the direction the metal is bent."

"Makes no difference," said Toribio. "Bullets can ricochet. I say a bullet from Ernesto's rifle hit something near my truck, ricocheted into the window, and out through the roof."

Papá and Toribio argued about thirty minutes over the ricocheting bullet theory. Toribio threatened to complain to the sheriff about Papá's reckless sons. Finally Papá offered Toribio ten dollars, which he quickly accepted. Toribio then jumped into his damaged pickup truck, waved good-bye to me and Ernesto, and headed to town.

I thought about that day as I stood alone on the canal bank with Ernesto's rifle and looked across the fields toward Toribio's house. I didn't want to take a chance of putting another bullet into Toribio's Studebaker pickup or, even worse, into Toribio, so I decided to go to the *monte* to shoot the rifle.

Before entering the dark *monte,* I loaded the rifle and slid the safety latch into place. I started slowly down the path, stopping every few feet to listen. The *monte* was quiet, no sounds could be heard from outside the thick stand of mesquite and *huisache.* I think this was part of the fascination I had always felt for the *monte.* It shut out the world and allowed an escape from life's ordinary routines. It was large enough to be a little frightening and was known to harbor wildlife, such as armadillos and javelinas. When Papá was a youngster he saw deer and ocelots there, but I had never seen anything but snakes, opossums, raccoons, and rats.

As I arrived at the clearing where Señorita Sinforosa's house once stood, I saw a javelina across the clearing at the edge of the brush. I stopped and shouldered the rifle, slipped off the safety, and aimed. I squeezed the trigger just as Ernesto had taught me. The rifle fired, the javalina jumped up in the air, landed on its feet, and ran into the brush. I was sure that I had hit it, so I ran after it. I could hear it grunting as it crashed through the brush ahead of me, but I couldn't keep up with it because the cacti were becoming too dense and treacherous. Deciding to let the animal go, I turned and began to retrace my steps.

Before I reached the clearing, I heard the javalina moving nearby. I began going through the thick brush toward where I thought it was. I had not gone far when I tripped over something in the undergrowth. I jumped up and pushed the brush aside. There lay a man on his back, apparently dead from the bullet that had made the hole in the middle of his forehead. I was horrified. How could I have shot him? I was sure I had hit the javalina. This man was nowhere near the javalina. I thought of Toribio's ricochet theory and began running home as fast as I could.

Papá was in the field plowing. I ran to him with the rifle held high above my head.

"Papá, Papá, I've shot a man in the *monte*! I didn't mean to do it!" I was so out of breath that Papá didn't seem to understand me.

He stopped the mules and pulled his bandana away from his nose and mouth. "*Cálmate*, and tell me what you've done," Papá said as he freed himself from the reins.

"I shot a man in the *monte*," I repeated. "It was an accident." I set the rifle down in a furrow.

Papá began running toward the *monte* with me following. As we ran, I tried to explain to him about the javalina, but I think I was so terribly frightened that I couldn't run and talk well at the same time.

We entered the *monte* and soon arrived at the clearing. I hesitated because I didn't want to see the dead man again.

"Where is he, *mi'jo*, show me?" Papá grabbed my arm. "Where is the man you shot?"

I took Papá through the brush until I could barely see the man's body lying where I had left him. "Over there, Papá," I said and pointed.

Papá hurried over to the body. I couldn't bear to watch anymore, so I went back to the clearing and waited for Papá.

Papá didn't take long to examine the dead man.

"How did you say you killed that man?" Papá asked with a strange look on his face.

"With Ernesto's rifle I shot at a javalina, and I guess I missed it and shot that man, or the bullet ricocheted."

"When did this happen?" Papá still had that look on his face.

"Just a little while ago, just before I told you about it."

"You didn't kill that man. He's been dead for a while, at least since yesterday or the day before." Papá's face seemed normal again. "But you had no right to take Ernesto's rifle. I'm very disappointed in you."

"*Lo siento,* Papá. Ernesto taught me to use the rifle. He told me that when he bought a new one he would give me the old one." I didn't say anymore because Papá had turned his back on me and was walking out of the *monte*.

We returned to the mule team, which hadn't moved since Papá and I had left. Papá told me he had to go into town to report to the sheriff about finding the dead man. He picked up Ernesto's rifle and left me to finish the plowing.

That night at our evening meal, the dead man was the topic of conversation. Everyone wanted to hear the gruesome details of my adventure in the *monte*. Papá said I should have known by the bad odor that I couldn't have killed the man. I said that I never smelled an odor. The coroner substantiated that the man had been dead for several days. The man also had three bullets in his body. I was relieved that I had not been responsible for his death. According to the sheriff, the man was a stranger to our area and probably had been killed and robbed.

Before going to bed that night, Papá came out to the sleeping house. He had Ernesto's rifle with him.

"Miguel, I'm giving you this rifle," Papá said as he held out Ernesto's rifle.

"I don't want it," Miguel said and frowned.

"You're the eldest son now; it must go to you." Papá attempted again to hand it to Miguel who was lying across the bed.

"I said I don't want it." Miguel stood up. "I don't ever want to kill animals. They should be left alone." Miguel pointed at me. "Give the rifle to him. He wants to kill things."

Papá moved closer to Miguel. "I don't want Alejandro to have it. I want my eldest son to have it. So take it." Papá thrust the rifle into Miguel's hands and walked out of the sleeping house.

That night I had difficulty going to sleep. I thought a lot about the dead man and about Ernesto's rifle. I also thought a lot about how fortunate it must be to be the eldest son.

XIV

For the Love of the Game

I was nearly grown before I ever saw a television set. For many years there weren't any television stations south of San Antonio, and we were too far away to pick up the signals. Television finally came to deep South Texas, but it didn't come to our house. My parents decided that a television set was something that we could do without.

"I don't want one of those noisy things in my house," said Mamá as she shook her head, "especially after visiting with Doña Amelia González last week. That television set of theirs was so noisy and distracting that we couldn't even visit."

"I don't want a television set either," said Papá. "They're too expensive, and we have too much work around here to do. We don't have time for such frivolous pastimes." He gulped down the remainder of the coffee in his cup and went out the door.

I wanted a television set and so did Miguel, Rosa, and Virginia. Now that we had electricity at Chicken Foot Farm, we wanted many new appliances and devices, with the television being number one on our list.

Toribio Tovar, who always said he was too poor to modernize his farming, was the first one in the area to spend money on a television set. He added to our covetousness by telling us,

"TV is great! You *chamacos* just don't know what you're missing, like baseball, boxing, and all kinds of shows. Yes, you definitely need a TV."

He didn't invite us to see his, and it looked as if we weren't going to get a television set of our own. So I was happy to hear that the González's had one. They lived near us, and their son Manny was a good friend of Miguel. So, I excitedly approached Miguel. "*Hermano*, did you know that the González family bought a television set?"

"Sure I know. I saw it last week when I was there with Manny," Miguel nonchalantly answered.

"Well, do you think you could take me with you the next time you go visit him? I really want to see what television is like."

"I'm going over on Saturday to watch baseball. You can come if you want," Miguel said.

I was thrilled at the prospect of seeing baseball players running around in a little box. That was almost unimaginable. When Saturday came, I did my chores with a renewed exuberance just knowing that soon I would be sitting with Manny in his living room watching my favorite sport.

Upon arriving at Manny's, we found him already settled in front of the television. Manny's parents weren't home, but several of his sisters were in the kitchen. Miguel and I quickly said hello and seated ourselves in the living room.

I was so excited to watch television for the first time that I think I didn't detect the offensive odor at first. Soon, however, an aroma of stinky feet began to demand my attention. I looked around the small room. Miguel and I were sitting on the sofa with our shoes on. Manny was seated in an armchair with his bare feet propped up on a small ottoman. Next to the ottoman sat his work shoes and socks. No one else was in the room, so I knew it had to be Manny's feet. I tried to concentrate on the game, which I was enjoying tremendously, however the intrusive odor did occasionally diminish my pleasure.

Shortly before the game was over, Manny's older brother Rigo came home. He walked into the living room, wrinkled his nose, and said to Manny, "*¡Qué pies tan apestosos!* Put your shoes back on!"

Manny paid no attention and continued watching the game. I thought it would be more socially appropriate on my part to totally ignore what had just been said. I looked at Miguel who seemed to be clenching his teeth to keep from bursting out in laughter. The game was over shortly, and it was a relief to get out of the González's house. At that moment, I wasn't sure if I could ever return, no matter how much I loved baseball.

The next Saturday Miguel asked me to go with him to Manny's to watch a baseball game. I went with him although I wasn't eager for a repeat performance of Manny's stinky feet, but that was exactly what we got.

"What's wrong with Manny? Why can't he wash his feet before we get together to watch TV?" I asked Miguel after we had left Manny's house.

"I don't know. Maybe Manny's lazy," Miguel replied and shrugged his shoulders.

"Well, perhaps it would help if he'd just remove his smelly shoes and socks from the living room," I said.

"I've told him that his feet stink and not to take his shoes off while we're watching the game, but he doesn't seem to care. He said it was his TV and he could watch it however he liked."

"Well, tell him again," I said.

"I don't think that will do any good. It's going to take a little more than that."

"Maybe we should tell his mother," I said.

"Sure, you go ahead and tell Doña Amelia," Miguel said and laughed.

Miguel knew that I couldn't bring myself to do that. I'd rather pick Manny up, throw him in the irrigation ditch, and wash his feet myself.

"There's nothing we can do," I said. "We'll just have to endure the stench of his feet if we want to watch television. I can put up with it, I guess."

"I have an idea," Miguel responded with a slight smile.

On the next Saturday morning I overheard Miguel talking to Rosa.

"Go today with me and Alejandro to Manny's house to watch television," Miguel said.

"I don't think I want to go. I don't care much for those González boys," Rosa replied and turned back to the tortilla she was rolling.

"Well, too bad you don't want to go. Their sister Gloria asked me to bring you," Miguel said.

"My goodness, *hermano*, you hardly ever offer to take me anywhere with you. And why is Gloria González inviting me to her house?" Rosa asked with an apparent tone of suspicion in her voice.

Well, I was wondering also. I hadn't heard Gloria González tell Miguel to bring Rosa with him.

"Just go with us today," Miguel said and smiled at Rosa. "I want you to check out the television. You said you'd like to watch TV and this is your chance."

"Yes, you're right about that. I really would like to watch TV. I think I'll go with you." Rosa began rolling the tortillas a little faster than usual.

When Miguel and I were alone, I said, "You're lying. I don't think Gloria invited Rosa. What's the real reason Rosa's going with us?"

"Don't you know?" Miguel said and grinned. "Manny likes Rosa. Maybe she can cure his stinky feet."

Rosa was the first one ready to go to Manny's. She had a bag of ginger pig cookies in her hand to take to the González family. There was something about her that didn't look quite usual. She had curled her hair, put on her best dress, and borrowed Virginia's new shoes. I even noted pink color on her cheeks and lips.

Miguel had a strange little look on his face when he said, "You didn't need to go to so much trouble, *hermana*, just to see a baseball game on television."

"What are you talking about? I didn't go to any trouble, and if you say anything about my hair, I'm staying home." Rosa climbed into the cab of the pickup and said nothing more.

When we arrived at the González's house, Manny was already seated in the big armchair with his bare feet propped up on the ottoman. When he saw that Rosa was with us, he didn't even say hello. He jumped up, grabbed his shoes and socks, and left the room.

Rosa went into the kitchen to visit with Gloria and Doña Amelia, and Miguel and I sat down in our usual places to enjoy the game. There was a faint odor of feet but it soon dissipated. When Manny returned he appeared clean and dressed in fresh clothing including clean socks and shined shoes. I noticed that Miguel seemed somewhat exuberant during the entire game, laughing and chuckling from time to time.

Manny got up and went to the kitchen a number of times. This was unusual as he hadn't done that during the other occasions when we had watched television with him. I could hear Manny talking to Rosa who had stayed in the kitchen. Miguel must have been right. Manny liked Rosa. But Rosa didn't like Manny, or did she?

For the rest of the summer, Miguel and I went over to Manny's house almost every Saturday. Rosa went with us on many of those occasions. It got to the point that no one had to invite her, and I think she just assumed that she was going. In fact, she seemed to look forward to her visits to the González's house. Rosa's presence must have made the difference because we never again had to smell Manny's stinky feet.

Perhaps Rosa had to smell them because she and Manny were married about six months after television came into our lives. The newlyweds eventually moved to Robstown where Manny got a good-paying job in the oil field. Rosa was so homesick that she wanted to come home every time Manny had two or three days off. Manny soon got tired of that, so he quit his job and found a new one in Odessa, which was too far away for Rosa to come home very often. I heard that Manny bought her a big television set in a nice mahogany cabinet to keep her from feeling lonely and homesick. What a lucky girl.

XV

A Kitchen Calamity

Gordon Fisher had been sitting in our kitchen for most of the morning. He and Papá were discussing farming while they ate the breakfast that Virginia had prepared. I sat at the end of the table eating an egg and *chorizo* taco. I listened as the men's conversation turned to Gordon's old Case tractor that he was offering to sell to Papá.

"I know she's old and the paint's faded," said Gordon, "but she'll still give you a few years of service." He pushed his empty plate toward the end of the table and smiled at Virginia who was standing near the stove watching Gordon.

Papá cleaned his mouth with his blue bandana. "I really need a tractor. I should have bought one by now. But the prices are just too high." Then he paused and nodded his head toward Virginia. "She's a very good cook."

Gordon smiled. Virginia's face turned red, and she turned around and began wiping the sideboard with a dish towel.

"Well, Don Sigifredo, then it's settled. I'll bring her down this afternoon." Gordon picked up his straw hat that was lying on the bench beside him, and he stood up to leave. He hesitated and looked toward Virginia who was standing with her back to him. "Thanks for breakfast, Virginia."

Virginia didn't say a word or turn around. I felt rather sorry for Gordon because he was always very courteous to Virginia, and she usually ignored him. And sometimes she was terribly rude to him. Papá wanted Virginia to marry Gordon because he thought she would have a good life with Gordon. When he inherited his grandmother's land, he would be a wealthy farmer.

"Did you buy Gordon's old tractor, Papá?" I was so excited that I was talking with my mouth full of food.

"Yes, *era una ganga*, only three hundred dollars. *Fíjate, mi'jo*, my first tractor. Now I can cultivate several rows at a time." Papá smiled.

I hadn't seen Papá appear this happy in a long time. Gordon had made it very easy to buy the tractor, with nothing down and the balance to be paid over the next three crops. Yes, it was a bargain. I was sure that Gordon's old tractor was worth a lot more than three hundred dollars. But, of course, he was in love with Virginia.

That afternoon, as Gordon had promised, he drove his old tractor down to Chicken Foot Farm. Papá, Abuelo Angel, and I were the first ones to welcome the tractor. It seemed larger up close than it did when I had seen Gordon driving it across Madama Fisher's fields.

"Well, Don Sigifredo, do you want to drive it?" Gordon jumped down from the seat.

Papá seemed a little reluctant, but he climbed up onto the tractor. Gordon instructed Papá about operating it, and then Papá began driving it out toward the equipment shed with Gordon following on foot.

"I guess we'll have to sell the mules now, unless you want to eat them, Alejandro," Abuelo Angel said and laughed.

Poor mules, who would want them? A lot of the farmers were buying tractors. "Who do you think would want to buy the mules?" I asked.

"Probably Toribio Tovar will buy one or both of them," Abuelo Angel responded. "He says he can't afford a tractor."

Papá had turned the tractor around and was now coming back to where Abuelo Angel and I stood not far from the kitchen. I wanted to learn to drive the tractor. This was something that I thought I could easily do to help Papá more, and he would be proud of me.

I walked over to the tractor just as Papá brought it to a stop. "I want to learn to drive it, Papá."

"Not now, Alejandro. Miguel must learn to operate this machine. Go find him."

I found Miguel in our sleeping house assembling a model airplane.

"Papá wants you to come out and learn to drive the tractor," I said.

Miguel frowned. "I don't want to learn to drive it. You know I don't intend to be a farmer."

Miguel complained a lot about the work Papá had us do. Driving the mule team was hard labor, but we had to do it. Miguel and I had begun helping with the cotton picking by the time we were eight or nine years old. Abuela Luciana had made us little burlap bags to drag along the rows for collecting the cotton. When the bags got too heavy, we emptied them into the nearest adult's bag. At the end of the day, Mamá rubbed bay rum and glycerin on the cuts on our fingers caused by the sharp boll hulls. I knew farming would be much easier now with the purchase of Gordon's tractor, but it would still be hard work.

I heard Papá's voice angrily yelling for Miguel to come learn to drive the tractor. We both hurried out of the sleeping house, and Miguel was soon up on the tractor seat.

"I don't think I should do this, Papá. I don't understand these controls," Miguel said as he attempted to put the tractor in gear.

"It's easy. Just do it the way Gordon showed you," Papá said.

"Let me drive it, Papá. I think I can do it," I said.

I guess Papá couldn't hear me over the noise of the tractor's engine.

"*Mi'jo*, you must learn," Papá said to Miguel. "You're my eldest son now." Papá raised his arm and moved it in a sweeping motion and said, "This will all be yours someday. Now learn to drive the tractor!"

Miguel put the tractor in gear, and it began moving across the yard. He didn't go very far before he turned the tractor around and headed back toward us.

"Turn the wheel! Turn the wheel!" Papá yelled at Miguel who seemed to be going straight toward the kitchen.

Miguel didn't turn the wheel.

"Turn off the engine! Turn off the engine!" Gordon yelled.

Miguel didn't turn off the engine. The tractor hit the front corner of the kitchen causing most of the roof and two walls of the structure to come crashing down. A piece of two-by-four flew out of the framework and hit Miguel in the forehead, knocking him off of the tractor. Gordon jumped up on the tractor and stopped it. By the time Gordon got the tractor moved back from the pile of rubble that had been the kitchen, Mamá and Virginia had reached Miguel. He was sitting on the ground holding his head in his hands.

The scene I was viewing was almost comical. Papá and Gordon were inspecting the front end of the tractor. Mamá and Virginia were inspecting the forehead of Miguel, and Abuelo Angel was hopping around yelling, "Luciana! Luciana!"

It took a few moments before I realized that Abuela Luciana was somewhere under the ruins of the kitchen. There was only one entrance to the kitchen, and it was gone with the destroyed wall. I rushed around to the back wall of the kitchen that was still standing, and I pulled off some loose boards so I could squeeze through. There she sat at the table where she had been cleaning beans, my dear abuela, with the kitchen's roof hanging about two inches above her head. She said nothing but looked at me with both of her eyebrows raised. The roof and remaining walls were swaying and making creaking sounds. I got Abuela Luciana back to the hole in the wall just as Abuelo Angel pulled off more boards to make it easier for us to get out.

I seated Abuela Luciana in an old wooden chair under the fresno tree. She seemed a little shaky, but she didn't appear to have been injured in any way. She crossed herself and began to bless the kitchen just as the remaining walls and roof came crashing down with a loud boom.

Mamá cleaned the blood off of Miguel's forehead with her blue lace-trimmed handkerchief. Miguel said he felt fine.

"Look what you've done to my tractor!" Papá said to Miguel.

"Look what you've done to our kitchen!" Virginia said.

"You almost killed your grandmother!" said Abuelo Angel.

Papá yelled many bad words at Miguel who sat on the ground holding Mamá's blue handkerchief against the cut in his forehead. Papá's face turned very red as he circled Miguel, stomping his feet and thrashing his arms as he told my brother how inept he was at becoming a farmer.

Mamá finally intervened. *"Por el amor de Dios*, Sigifredo, stop it before you give yourself a heart attack!"

Papá stopped and, gasping for air, told Miguel to get back on the tractor.

Miguel stood up and spat on the ground. "I said I didn't want to learn to drive a tractor, and I'm not going to do it." He walked away toward the sleeping house.

That evening Miguel left Chicken Foot Farm and went to live with Tío Onécimo in San Antonio. He took with him Ernesto's rifle. I never understood why he did that. He also took all of Mamá's egg and chicken money that she kept in the lard can on top of her chifforobe. He didn't steal it; Mamá gave it to him along with her blessings. She said the money would help him get a new start in life. Papá said she should have kept her money to help pay for the new kitchen we were going to have to build.

Without the kitchen, our evening meal couldn't be prepared, so Papá and Abuelo Angel went into town for a few groceries. They brought back several loaves of sliced bread, cold cuts, coffee, *pan dulce*, and a big glass jar of pickled lambs' tongues. I pulled the enamel coffeepot out of the rubble and made a small fire on the ground so Virginia could boil some coffee. We had only three coffee cups among us because that was all I could find without crawling farther under the fallen roof. Abuelo Angel and I made a temporary table with plywood and set it under the fresno tree. We gathered old benches and chairs from the yard to sit on.

After our evening meal, we all walked over to the collapsed kitchen to discuss how we would proceed with the clearing away of the rubble and restoring the structure.

"*Ay, Virgen santa*, our poor kitchen. Now what shall we do?" said Mamá with tears in her eyes as she stood looking at the pile of broken pieces of lumber and twisted sections of tin roofing.

Papá patted Mamá on the arm as he said, "We'll build a new one of thick, heavy lumber. One with big windows and a roof with shingles. It'll be strong and well built and will last for years. Nothing will ever destroy it."

Mamá smiled and wiped the tears from her eyes.

Abuela Luciana began making signs of the cross to bless us. *"Dios los bendiga, Dios los bendiga,"* she repeated over and over. Then she walked over to the fallen kitchen. I was sure she was going to bless it too. But she turned to us smiling and said, *"¿Saben qué?* I never really liked this kitchen. It was always too hot and stuffy, and the metal roof made lots of noise."

XVI

The Migrant

"No, you can't go to work for Madama Fisher. I have enough work for you here," said Papá without looking at me. He was working on his tractor engine, which was giving him trouble again.

"But Papá, I'm seventeen years old. I want to earn my own money. Madama Fisher will give me money to work."

Papá said nothing and continued with what he was doing.

"Papá, please, I want to work for Madama Fisher. I don't want to work for you. You never pay me." I kicked up some dirt with the toe of my shoe.

Papá stopped what he was doing and turned around to face me. "Pay you? Why should I pay you, *mi'jo*? I provide what you need—your food, a house to live in, everything. You should be happy working for me."

I didn't have the courage to tell him of the times I wanted to buy myself new shoes or a new shirt, but didn't have any money. Usually, I didn't even have money to buy myself a Coke or a hamburger when I went into town.

I lowered my head, not knowing for sure what to say. "*Bueno*, Papá. *Lo siento*." I walked away.

Looking across the compound, I saw Tío Erasmo's sons loading their big blue farm truck in preparation for the trip to

California to work in the vegetable and fruit harvests. For several years, Tío Erasmo and his family had been migrating west, usually leaving in the spring and returning to Chicken Foot Farm in the fall. My uncle had often asked Papá to let me go, but Papá always said there was more than enough work for me at home.

I wanted to say good-bye to Cándido and Roque before they left for California, so I walked over to their house. I saw that my uncle was covering his house windows as he did every year before leaving.

"Come with us, Alejandro," Tío Erasmo said as he drove a nail into a piece of plywood that he had placed over a window. "It's almost June. You should be able to go with us. Isn't your school out for the summer?"

"Yes, but I can't go with you. Papá will not allow it." I picked up the coffee can that held the nails and followed my uncle around to the back of their house. I could hear Tía Inocencia's loud voice coming from inside the house as she gave out assignments to her sons.

Tío Erasmo stopped at an uncovered window. "I've often told your father that you should come along to California so you could make lots of money to bring home to him. But he always says you can't go. Your father is *cabezudo* and a very proud man."

"He wants me to work all the time because that's all he does." I held a large piece of plywood in place across the window for my uncle. In my head, I agreed with Tío Erasmo. My dad was hardheaded.

Tío Erasmo began hammering nails into the wood and then paused. "We all know how hard your father works to be a good provider for his family. I think he has needed to prove to the Martínez family that he was worthy of your mother."

I looked down at the ground.

Tío Erasmo finished nailing the wood across the window. "Yes, those Martínezes, especially your grandmother Martínez, thought that your mother was too good to marry a farmer. Did you know that your grandmother called your father a no-good *lobo jambujo* and said her daughter would never marry him?"

I had heard this story before. I handed my uncle the nail can. "Well, Mamá *did* marry him. And just what is a *lobo jambujo* anyway?"

"I'm afraid I don't know. Only your Grandmother Martínez knows and she's dead."

I decided to go home and talk to Papá about going to California with Tío Erasmo. Papá was alone at the table eating a late supper. He didn't look up at me when I walked into the kitchen. Mamá smiled at me and continued washing dishes.

"I want to go to California with Tío Erasmo, just for the summer." I stood at the table looking down at Papá who was eating *frijoles refritos* with pieces of tortilla that he formed into little scoops.

Papá continued scooping up his beans and didn't look up at me. "You cannot go."

"Papá, please, can't we talk about it?"

Papá dropped a tortilla scoop full of beans back down into his plate. He looked up at me, swallowed, and said, "No, we cannot talk about it. There is nothing to talk about." Then he looked down at his plate, picked up a piece of tortilla, and continued eating.

I said nothing and left the kitchen and walked out to the fresno tree where I sat down on the ground and thought over what had just transpired. I wasn't surprised at Papá's response. He and I seldom discussed anything. He talked to me only when he needed to give me information or to scold me. If I pleased him, he never said so, and he never seemed happy when I was around him.

One time I had said to Papá, "Why don't you ever say anything to me when I do something good? You're always quick to criticize me when I do things wrong."

He answered, "I shouldn't have to say anything when you do what is expected of you. But it is my duty to scold you when you do something wrong."

He wouldn't let me work for Madama Fisher, and he wouldn't allow me to go with Tío Erasmo. This made me angry and hurt, so I made the decision that I would go to California without his permission. I would earn a lot of money, come home, and give it all to him. Then Papá would be so pleased that he wouldn't be upset with me for going without his permission.

It was after dark when I went out to the sleeping house and put a few of my things into a large brown paper bag. I rushed to Tío Erasmo's house and climbed up and over the side panel of the big truck, just as it was leaving Chicken Foot Farm.

I wasn't the only passenger in the back of the truck. Besides my cousins, Roque and Cándido, five members of the Silva family were huddled together in one corner. By the light of the moon I could see the ugly Moreno brothers, Celedonio and Petrolino. They were sprawled out across a dirty mattress that Tío Erasmo usually carried in the back of his truck for long trips. My cousins acknowledged me, but the Moreno brothers made a snorting sound and looked away. They never seemed to like me after the time Papá had hired them and fired them a few days later because of their laziness.

I ignored the Moreno brothers and settled back against the high side panel for what I knew would be a long trip. I began to feel hungry, and I imagined that Tía Inocencia was in the truck cab seated beside Tío Erasmo, eating all kinds of cookies and candies and other treats that she kept only for herself.

We rode for hours without stopping. The Moreno brothers seemed to be able to sleep soundly in the truck with its wooden side panels rattling loudly. Roque and Cándido laughed and played and wrestled around on the floor like little boys instead of teenagers. The Silva family sat in a tight cluster and mumbled to each other in low voices. I slept part of the night and awakened before daylight. Sometime during the morning we stopped at a grimy-looking gasoline station somewhere in West Texas.

"*Bueno, gente*, get out and stretch your legs," Tío Erasmo called to us as he, with Cándido's help, lowered the end panel. He noticed me. "I saw you in the mirror when you jumped into the truck last night. What did your Papá say about you coming with me?"

"Nothing, I didn't tell him." I got down from the truck.

Tía Inocencia walked up to me wagging her fat finger in my face. "And your poor, poor Mother, does she know where you are?"

I winced but said nothing.

"*Pobre* Ramona. What has she ever done to deserve *un hijo desgraciado* like you?" Tía Inocencia sneered and walked away.

The station attendant began filling the truck's large fuel tank with gasoline, and I walked toward the building to find a toilet.

"You have to use the privy way out in the back," the attendant called to me.

I walked around to the back and saw a decrepit outhouse located on a small knoll with a line of Silvas waiting to use it. The Moreno brothers were standing behind the outhouse relieving themselves. After the Silvas, Tía Inocencia had to use the privy, and then Cándido and then Roque. Finally I got into the outhouse, and, as I sat there, I prayed that Tío Erasmo would know where I was and would not leave me. But when I emerged from the outhouse, the blue truck was nowhere in sight. I was aghast. I had not even heard the truck engine.

"What happened, boy? Did that bunch go off and leave you?" The attendant looked at me with a surprised look on his face when I walked into the station building.

"I don't know what happened. I didn't hear the truck," I answered.

I didn't like the appearance of the attendant who was a short, stocky man with long greasy blond hair. His hands and arms were spotted with black grease and one of his eyelids drooped. I thought he looked mean and menacing, like a pirate. I hurried out to the edge of the highway and looked up and down the road. I didn't see the truck.

The day was warm. I reached into my pocket for a hand-kerchief to wipe the sweat from my face and eyes. I didn't have one. My handkerchiefs and other possessions that I had brought were in the paper bag in the back of the truck. I pulled out my shirt tail and wiped my face.

After I tucked my shirt tail back in, I looked around at the surroundings. This wasn't a town, just a couple of gasoline sta-tions, a few houses, and some abandoned buildings. This didn't look like a good situation, especially with me not having any money. I was beginning to feel very hungry. I walked back to the station building and stood in the doorway. There was a rack on the counter with small bags of potato chips, corn chips, and some other food I didn't recognize. The attendant was standing inside the building looking at me.

"Well, just bide your time, boy. I reckon they'll miss you soon and come back for you." The attendant smiled and walked away.

For several hours I sat outside in the shade of the building watching some goats browsing on a rocky outcrop across the road from the station. This part of Texas seemed desolate and abandoned to me, and I was beginning to feel that I must have appeared the same way.

The attendant came outside and stood in the shade beside me. "Where are you from?"

"I live in the Lower Rio Grande Valley, and I wish I was back there now."

"Well, if you want, you can wave down the bus that comes by here around seven tonight. It goes all the way to Brownsville." The attendant picked at a scab on his arm. "It only costs four or five dollars."

I looked at the attendant and then looked quickly away because his drooping eyelid was quivering and that bothered me. "I don't have any money."

"That's too bad." The attendant started to go back inside but stopped and said, "If your people don't come back for you soon, I'll see if I can find you a ride. There should be some trucks stopping here that are going down to your part of the Valley."

A few vehicles stopped at the station, but they were all going the wrong way for me. I kept moving around the building to find shade as the sun rose higher and higher. My stomach was burning from hunger, and I kept thinking of the potato and egg tacos that I assumed Tía Inocencia had brought along for her breakfast this morning.

"Come on in, boy, and get out of the sun." The attendant motioned for me. "You must be hungry." He handed me a Coca Cola and a bag of peanuts.

I was very thankful, and I told him so. I quickly devoured the peanuts. Just as I was finishing the Coca Cola, Tío Erasmo's truck pulled up beside the gasoline pump. The Silvas, the Moreno brothers, and my cousins all jumped out of the truck and headed for the privy. I walked out to the truck.

Tía Inocencia slid down from the passenger side yelling, "Three and a half hours wasted!"

I stopped and faced her.

"And now three and a half more to get back to where we had to turn around. What's wrong with you? Are you stupid?" Tía Inocencia was yelling and coming at me with her fat index finger as usual.

"I'm sorry. I was in the privy." I began walking backward as Tía Inocencia by now was drumming on my chest with her finger.

Tío Erasmo walked up. "I didn't know you weren't in the back," he said with an apologetic look on his face.

"Who told you that I was missing? Was it Cándido?" I asked.

"No. It was Petrolino who told me we needed to come back for you," answered Tío Erasmo.

One of the Moreno brothers; I was shocked that he had done that for me.

Tío Erasmo continued, "He banged on the top of the cab until I stopped. I don't know why he waited so long."

"They all thought that you were in the cab with us," said Tía Inocencia as she finally relaxed her index finger. "You've cost us an entire day and lots of gasoline. You really owe us some money."

"And that's not all," said Petrolino who had just walked up with his brother. "We're going to miss one whole day of work because of you." He threw a candy bar wrapper on the ground, which landed near my feet. "You'll owe me and Celedonio one day's wages each."

"And you'll owe us lost wages, too." Tía Inocencia started to raise her finger but stopped and put her hands on her hips. "You'll be working all summer just to pay for the big mistake you made. The Silvas will also have to be paid."

"I think I'd just rather go back home," I said. "There's a bus at seven tonight but I don't have any money." I looked around for Tío Erasmo, but he was buying soda pops.

Then, Tía Inocencia did something that I would have never thought she was capable of doing. She reached inside her blouse and pulled out a dingy white handkerchief knotted into a small bundle. She untied the knot, took a ten-dollar bill from a wad of money, and handed it to me.

"Take this and go home. Your poor Mother is probably sick with worry." Tía Inocencia turned around and began walking in the direction of the privy.

I was glad not to be in the truck when it left the gasoline station. As the truck pulled on to the highway, I saw Celedonio Moreno hanging over the side panel with my forgotten paper bag in his hand. He laughed as he dangled it over the side of the truck, then he quickly pulled it into the truck after him. I never saw him or the bag again.

That night I flagged down the bus and arrived home late the next afternoon. When I walked into the kitchen Mamá was alone cleaning the milk separator. She looked up at me, said nothing, and continued with her work. Instead of acting happy or relieved to see me, she ignored me as if she were angry.

"Mamá, *lo siento mucho*. I'm so sorry."

"Well, tell it to your father. He's the one you have hurt." She turned her back on me.

I rushed out of the kitchen and stopped under the fresno tree. Tears began running down my face. I saw Papá coming toward me from the equipment shed. When he reached me he took me in his arms and held me.

In a halting voice, he said, "First Ernesto is killed. Then Miguel leaves me. Yesterday I thought I had lost you, too." He attempted to say something else, but his voice broke.

I saw tears in his eyes as he turned me loose and walked away. We never spoke of this again, but that didn't matter. What mattered is that it happened.

XVII

Squash Blossoms

"Alejandro, come quickly and help me find your grandmother," Mamá said as she rushed into the kitchen.

I was searching through the cupboard for the fig newtons. "Isn't she in her house?"

"No, I've looked there and all around the other buildings." Mamá walked back to the kitchen entrance and looked out across the family compound. "Your father and grandfather are still in town. I wish they were here."

I knew it would probably be hours before Papá and Abuelo Angel would come home. It was Saturday, the day those two went into town to buy the family provisions.

"I'm worried, *mi'jo*." Mamá reached out and touched my arm. "Please hurry."

I decided to forego my snack for the moment. "Where do you suppose Abuela Luciana has gone?"

"I have no idea. I sent Virginia to look for her at Madama Fisher's." Mamá untied her apron and put it across the back of a chair. "I'm very concerned about her."

We left the kitchen and began searching the compound. I understood Mamá's uneasiness. Abuela Luciana's behavior of late had become strange. Often her talk was senseless. She burned a lot of tortillas and sometimes forgot to add water to the boiling beans. Mamá and Virginia wanted to take over all of the cooking, but Abuela Luciana refused to allow that. I noticed that my grandmother often fell asleep at the kitchen table.

"I'm not asleep. I'm just resting my eyes," she would sternly say if anyone accused her of napping.

"I think Abuela Luciana is becoming senile," Virginia had told me. "She seems confused about things, like she's lost. Last week she told me that the privy had been moved. I assured her that it was still in the same place."

I thought about the privy. "Mamá, did you look in the privy?" I turned and pointed toward the outside toilet.

"Yes, three times. She wasn't there. I'll look again."

I headed toward the equipment shed thinking that Abuela Luciana may have gone there in search of Abuelo Angel. As I passed by the cactus fence that surrounded grandfather's vegetable garden, I faintly heard Abuela Luciana's thin falsetto voice. She was singing a song about a swallow that could not find its way back home.

"Mamá! Mamá! She's here in the vegetable garden!" I quickly opened the sagging gate and saw my barefoot grandmother sitting at the end of a row of squash plants. She was dressed in her old faded nightgown. Her white hair tumbled wildly around her shoulders.

I hurried to the end of the squash row and stood looking with astonishment at Abuela Luciana who sat encircled by squash blossoms. Some of the flowers were strewn across her nightgown. Some were adorning her hair, and others were arranged in small piles in front of her. Abuela Luciana continued singing her sad song as, one by one, she fashioned squash blossoms into a long yellow garland.

Mamá muffled a gasp with the palm of her hand. "*Por el amor de Dios*, Luciana! Look what you've done!" Mamá hurried to the end of the squash row. "You've picked all the flow-ers! Now we'll have no squash!"

Abuela Luciana looked up at Mamá and smiled, then resumed singing and making her garland.

"Mamá, what's wrong with Abuela Luciana? Why is she doing this?" I was startled by what I was observing.

"*Madre de Dios!* I don't know." Mamá bent over and flicked some of the squash blossoms off the top of my grand-mother's head. "Help me get her up and over to our house. *Ay*, this poor woman."

Abuela Luciana didn't protest, and Mamá soon had her in bed, where she slept until Abuelo Angel and Papá arrived home after dark.

After listening to Mamá's story of how we had found Abuela Luciana in the vegetable garden, Papá asked, "What do you think is wrong with my mother?"

"I'm not sure. Perhaps it's just old age," Mamá answered and shrugged her shoulders.

Abuelo Angel sat quietly by the bed, gently patting Abuela Luciana's hand. Finally he said, "Sigifredo, I want you to go into town and ask Dr. Mueller to please come."

We seldom needed Dr. Mueller because Abuela Luciana usually healed our family members with her herbs and special cures, and an occasional Watkins product. She was well known among the local farm families for her talent as a healer, and she gladly applied her skills to anyone that needed her. Now I feared that the *curandera* could not heal herself.

After examining Abuela Luciana, Dr. Mueller did not seem very concerned. He rummaged around in his black bag and chose a glass bottle containing a brown liquid. "Old age is catching up with her. That's all it is. She needs to rest and take this tonic every day." He reached again into his bag and took out a box of vitamin pills. "These are large tablets. Cut them into pieces so Doña Luciana can swallow them easily."

However, my grandmother never swallowed *any* of the medications.

"*Ay, Dios mío.* Don't give me that horrible medicine! I won't take it!" Abuela Luciana would cry out as she spit out any part of the vitamin tablet that Mamá was able to get into her mouth. Usually Abuela Luciana clenched her teeth and refused to open them for any of us.

Abuelo Angel would try desperately to get Abuela Luciana to take some of the tonic that the doctor had left. "Take this, Luciana. It's good for you," he would plea.

"No! That's poison from the devil! Get it away from me!" Abuela Luciana would push my grandfather away. "Why are all of you trying to kill me? Who has put *mal de ojo* on me? Was it you, Virginia?"

"No one has put a curse on you," Abuelo Angel would say quietly and would pat Abuela Luciana on the arm.

That did not placate her. Every day she yelled at us to get the curse removed from her. One day she went so far as to tell Papá to notify the sheriff that she had been the victim of Tía Inocencia and she wanted her arrested.

"Inocencia is in California. She's done nothing to you." Papá attempted to assure Abuela Luciana.

"You're wrong. I've seen her, and I've heard her at night up on the roof," my grandmother said.

Virginia usually cried when Abuela Luciana talked of being cursed. "How can she think such a thing? She's accusing Tía Inocencia who isn't even here. This is crazy, and I don't understand any of this."

"It must be a brain attack that has affected your grandmother. Her mind is very confused." Mamá spoke softly so only Virginia and I could hear. "We must keep her in our house so she can be watched closely."

Abuela Luciana refused to stay in bed; therefore, Virginia was assigned to monitor her as she moved about the compound. This arrangement worked well until the day that Abuela Luciana disappeared. It happened one afternoon just after I arrived home from school. Virginia accompanied Abuela Luciana to the outside privy. It was from the privy that she vanished.

"Why didn't you stay with her? How could you let this happen?" Mamá demanded to know.

"She never wants me to go in with her." Tears began to run down Virginia's face. "I walked over to sit in the shade of the laurel bush to wait for her."

"You shouldn't have left her," Mamá said and handed Virginia a handkerchief to wipe her eyes.

"The privy was never out of my sight. Mamá, I swear it!" Virginia began sobbing and threw herself onto the sofa.

"Virginia, quit your crying and go out to the fields and tell your father and grandfather that I need them. I'm going to Madama Fisher's to look for her." Mamá started toward the door, stopped, and turned to me. "Go look in the cistern. See if she has fallen in. If not, look in the canal."

I made a quick search of the cistern and canal. Then I made a round of the compound, including all of the buildings and the empty house where Tío Erasmo lived. Mamá returned from Madama Fisher's house without finding Abuela Luciana. By the time Papá and Abuelo Angel arrived at the compound, I was convinced that Abuela Luciana was not at Chicken Foot Farm.

We all met in the kitchen, and Abuelo Angel took charge of the search plans. "Sigifredo, drive up and down the roads. Your Mother may be walking to town."

"What can I do, Abuelo Angel? I feel so guilty that she's lost," Virginia said and wiped her red and swollen eyes.

"You can walk to the neighboring farms. See if anyone has seen her." Abuelo Angel then turned to Mamá and told her to stay in the compound in case Abuela Luciana returned.

"What about me?" I asked.

"You and I are going to the *monte*." Abuelo Angel left the kitchen with me following him.

We walked across the fields to the large stand of mesquite and *huisache* trees. The dense underbrush made it difficult to search anywhere except from the narrow paths that criss-crossed the dark and abandoned *monte*. It was in this thicket that I had shot at the javalina and found the dead man. Señorita Sinforosa's house had sat just inside of this dark *monte*. Now the house was gone, torn down by her nephews who took the salvaged lumber to sell.

I thought of Señorita Sinforosa as I followed Abuelo Angel down the path that led to where the old woman's house had stood. I remembered the night that Miguel and I had secretly watched her. "Abuelo, did you know that I once thought that Señorita Sinforosa was a witch?"

Abuelo Angel stopped and turned toward me. "A witch? What do you mean by a witch?"

"A person that can turn herself into black cats and put curses on people," I said.

Abuelo Angel laughed. "Sinforosa was an enchanting woman but never a witch." He turned and continued down the path. Suddenly he stopped. "Hurry! Let's go home. I think I know where your grandmother is."

After telling Mamá that we would return in about two hours, Abuelo Angel started the engine of his old farm truck. We headed down the narrow river road toward Tres Zopilotes.

The big truck bounced and rattled, making conversation difficult, but I wanted to know exactly where we were going. So I asked.

Abuelo Angel narrowed his eyes and said, "To the *jacal* of La Chimuela."

I had never seen La Chimuela, but I had passed by the little hut in which she lived. I knew of La Chimuela by her reputation. She was supposedly a *bruja*, a witch, and reportedly the best one in this part of Texas. At least that is what Abuela Luciana often said. She had known La Chimuela for many years and had consulted with her on several occasions.

I had recently heard Abuela Luciana say to Mamá, "You should go with me to visit La Chimuela. Everyone knows that she's very successful at what she does. And her Tarot readings are the best I've ever witnessed."

I noticed that Mamá bit her bottom lip before speaking. "You know I don't believe in that *tontería*." Mamá folded the dish towel she had been using, laid it on the table, and walked out of the kitchen leaving Abuela Luciana and me looking at one another.

My sisters also seemed to know about La Chimuela. I recalled that Rosa had told Virginia, "You need to go see La Chimuela. She'll give you an amulet to make a boy fall in love with you."

"*¡Cállate!* I can get a boyfriend by myself. I don't need that dirty old woman's dried-up hummingbirds!" Virginia had answered, apparently not happy with the suggestion that she needed help in attracting a boyfriend. She had certainly had more suitors than Rosa.

I pretended not to have heard that conversation, although the *bruja*'s hummingbirds caught my attention. Now, Abuelo Angel was driving us to the *jacal* of this well-known witch as fast as the old farm truck would allow.

It was almost dark when Abuelo Angel pulled the truck into the barren yard of a small hut on the outskirts of Tres Zopilotes. The entrance had no door, just a faded pink *colcha* hung across the doorway. A tall slender woman pulled back the *colcha*, which allowed the light of a lantern to shine out into the yard.

"Get down! Get down!" She yelled and motioned for us to come into her hut.

Rather than looking like a scary witch, I thought that the woman appeared rather ordinary with her black hair pulled up into a bun and a clean apron tied around her waist. In fact, she reminded me a little of Mamá's sister, Tía Pilar, only older.

La Chimuela gave us a big smile and continued holding the *colcha* aside so we could enter her hut. She held out her hand, which Abuelo Angel readily took. I greeted her in the same manner. A quick glance at her face told me why she was called La Chimuela. She was missing her front teeth, both uppers and lowers. I entered the hut expecting to find something terribly sinister. What I saw was Abuela Luciana sitting at a small wooden table drinking a cup of something that I thought must be tea. She looked up and smiled at Abuelo Angel and me.

La Chimuela walked over and stood behind Abuela Luciana's chair. "Welcome, Don Angel." Then she looked at me. "And you must be Alejandro. Doña Luciana has told me about you."

I attempted to smile but found it difficult in view of the fact that I had just bumped my head against a cluster of dried things hanging from a low roof support. Some of these may well have been hummingbirds. I looked around the hut. I saw a neatly made-up cot. Against the wall were several shelves with boxes and parcels on them. On a small table was a *molcajete*, the lava stone bowl used in grinding herbs and spices. I saw a stack of Tarot cards lying on the table near Abuela Luciana.

"Sit down, Don Angel," La Chimuela said as she pointed to an unpainted chair next to Abuela Luciana. Then she sat down on the other side of my grandmother. "I want to tell you about Doña Luciana's *mal de ojo*."

Abuelo Angel slowly sat down. "Yes, please tell me."

Because there were no more chairs, I stood standing next to the dried objects, waiting to hear what La Chimuela was going to say about my grandmother's evil eye curse.

La Chimuela cleared her throat and put her arm around Abuela Luciana's shoulders. "*Pobre de ella*, poor little lady. When Toribio Tovar brought her here, I could tell it was something bad. I've never seen Doña Luciana in such a terrible condition."

"So it was Toribio who gave her a ride," Abuelo Angel said and looked at me.

La Chimuela patted Abuela Luciana on the arm. "Yes, he found her walking along the road. She asked to be brought here to me." La Chimuela frowned and slowly shook her head. "You should have seen the inside of that egg, Don Angel." She paused and took a big breath. "It looked strange, sort of like the face of Satan, so I buried it." La Chimuela patted my grandmother on the arm. "I wish I had kept it to show you."

I also wished that she had kept it. I would have liked to have seen Satan's face. I was familiar with the egg treatment for *mal de ojo* because Abuela Luciana used this cure on family members and neighbors. She had even given Muggy Dan the egg treatment to remove freckles from her face. I don't think the treatment worked on Muggy Dan's freckles because there was nothing strange or uncommon looking about the egg when Abuela Luciana cracked it into a bowl of water. And, Muggy Dan never seemed to have a fewer amount of freckles. La Chimuela had said that the egg she used on Abuela Luciana appeared to have the face of Satan in it. I wondered how Abuelo Angel was going to respond to that.

Abuelo Angel didn't say anything about the egg with Satan's face. He simply said, "Thank you, I think I'll take my wife home now." Abuelo Angel arose and motioned to me to help him get Abuela Luciana up and out to the truck.

La Chimuela went to the doorway. "Yes, your wife was in terrible condition, but I was happy to help her. She kept insisting that her daughter-in-law, Erasmo's wife, had put a curse on her." La Chimuela pulled the *colcha* back for us. "What a sad situation."

Abuelo Angel stopped and took his brown leather coin purse out of his pocket. He gave La Chimuela 25 cents and thanked her again. We said very little on the bumpy trip back to Chicken Foot Farm. Abuela Luciana said she was hungry and wanted chicken *caldo* when we got home. Abuelo Angel said he wanted a cup of hot coffee.

"I want both," I said.

As the days passed after Abuela Luciana's trip to La Chimuela's hut, it was apparent that the treatment had made no difference in Abuela Luciana's condition. She continued to forget things, and she often seemed confused. However, I noticed that there was an appearance of serenity about her that I had not perceived before.

One afternoon after arriving home from school, I found Abuela Luciana alone in the kitchen.

"Are you hungry, Alejandro?" Abuela Luciana handed me a warm tortilla.

I sat down at the table and reached for the *melaza*. "Why does the table look different?" I asked as I dribbled the thick black syrup onto my tortilla.

"It's new oilcloth. I had your grandfather buy it today at the mercantile because the old one was wearing thin." Abuela

Luciana handed me a wet dishcloth to wipe the *melaza* off of my chin as she sat down across from me.

I looked at the oilcloth with its bright yellow flowers scattered over a blue background. "I like this new one."

Abuela Luciana smiled and rubbed the palms of her hands over the oilcloth. "So do I. Those are squash blossoms."

I reached across the table with my free hand and took one of Abuela Luciana's hands in mine and gently squeezed it. Perhaps this startled her because she quickly arose and rushed over to the stove. Maybe she was just burning another tortilla.

Three weeks later, Abuelo Angel awoke one morning to find that Abuela Luciana had passed away sometime during the night.

"We can be comforted in knowing that she left this world peacefully," Abuelo Angel told us.

I was very saddened to lose my dear grandmother, and I was terribly stressed at the prospect of losing Abuelo Angel also.

One evening when I was milking the cow, I said to him, "I'm afraid you're going to die soon, and I don't want that to happen."

"Why do you think that I'm going to die?" Abuelo Angel asked and put his hand on my shoulder.

"Because Abuela Luciana told me that it often happens to people when they have been married for many, many years. Don't you remember that Mamá Lola died soon after Abuelo Marcos's death?" I picked up the bucket of warm frothy milk.

"Listen to me, Alejandro. I think that happens only when people don't have much to live for." He motioned for us to start back to the kitchen. "I have lots to live for, like my grandchildren, and especially you."

"What do you mean?"

"I want to live to help you become a successful farmer. I want to make sure that you learn how to care for the land." He gently patted me on the back. "Already, you're doing a good job, and I'm proud of you."

My conversation with Abuelo Angel relieved me of my concern about his imminent death. He made me feel special, and above all, he gave me words of encouragement, something that I really needed.

XVIII

The Rescue of Little Cleofas

Tío Balde, who had married after moving to Brownsville, came back to live at Chicken Foot Farm. He brought with him his wife, Lorena, and two young sons. They moved into the house with Abuelo Angel. Tía Lorena was a small, frail-looking woman with a friendly nature. She smiled a lot and seemed to enjoy caring for my uncle and their children, Lito and Cleofas. However, not long after Tío Balde's return, the apparent peace and harmony of his family were suddenly disrupted by a situation that I overheard my parents discussing.

"She's taken Little Cleofas and left," Mamá said to Papá when he walked into the kitchen. "I predicted that she would leave your brother. And I don't blame her."

Mamá seemed to always know a lot about the happenings with Tío Balde and Tía Lorena because she and my aunt had become good friends.

I was sitting just outside the doorway cleaning the mud off of my work boots. I looked through the doorway and saw Mamá standing at the kitchen table making *masa* for tortillas in a big tin pan. I noted a tone of gravity in her voice.

"Well, did you already know that your sister-in-law left today?" Mamá pointed in the direction of Abuelo Angel's house.

"Yes, Balde told me this afternoon," Papá said as he washed his face and hands in the enamel basin on the washstand.

"And that's not all. *Pobre mujer*, she left here on foot carrying the boy and her suitcase to go all the way to the bus station in town." Mamá stepped back from the table and wiped her hands on her apron.

"She'll probably come back soon," Papá replied.

"I don't know why she would ever come back. Not after the way she's been treated by your brother." Mamá punched the ball of *masa* with her fist.

"Balde said Lorena talked bad to him. That's why he slapped her," Papá said.

"Lorena should have left both children for your brother to care for. I told her she should do that. That would have been a good lesson for Balde. Maybe then he would feel some appreciation and respect for Lorena."

I wanted to ask Mamá why Tía Lorena hadn't taken Lito also, but I decided not to say anything. I quietly came into the kitchen.

Mamá began to divide and shape the *masa* into small, round flat pieces, placing each one back into the tin pan.

"Add some wood to the stove, *mi'jo*," she said to me. She turned to Papá who had just sat down at the table with a steaming cup of coffee. "I guess this will teach your brother not to be mean to his wife. He deserves to lose her." She stirred the beans that were heating on the stove. "And what did your brother have to say about all of this?"

"He's not very pleased. Especially because she took little Cleofas," Papá answered.

Mamá shrugged her shoulders and began rolling tortillas. Papá quietly drank his coffee.

Later that evening Tío Balde came over to the kitchen with two bottles of beer in his hands. He and Papá sat alone in the kitchen, but I could see and hear everything because I sat in the darkness outside the doorway with Tío Balde's four-year-old son, Lito. It was obvious that Tío Balde was angry.

"I can't let Lorena get away with it," Tío Balde said as he set one of the bottles of beer in front of Papá. "Thank God she didn't take both of my sons. I would beat her for that. But, she had no right to take Cleofas." Tío Balde made a fist with one hand and punched it into the palm of his other hand.

Papá slowly shook his head and pushed the bottle of beer away. "*Cálmate, hermano.* Don't you suppose she took little Cleofas because he's not much more than a baby? How can you take care of such a young child?"

"Cleofas is my son. He belongs to me," Tío Balde replied.

"*Fíjate, hermano*, she left you your eldest son. He's the most important," Papá said. "He's the one that will take your place when you're gone."

"All sons are important, *hermano*! I think that's something you need to learn!" Balde hit his fist on the table, knocking both bottles of beer over.

Papá took his bandana from his back pocket and wiped up the beer.

Tío Balde seemed not to notice and pounded his fist again on the table. "You must go with me to Tres Zopilotes, *hermano*. I must get Cleofas back!"

"Why go there?" Papá asked.

"I'm certain that Lorena has gone to her sister's house. I'll force her to give the boy to me." Tío Balde took a deep breath. "I want you to go with me to get my son back. Please, *hermano*."

"Why don't you ask Erasmo to go?" Papá said.

Tío Balde arose from the table. "I did, but he won't go. Ever since he and Inocencia returned from California, he has complained about his knees and back hurting. He wouldn't be much good to me if he's physically weak." Tío Balde shrugged his shoulders. "You're all I have, *hermano*."

"*Bueno*," Papá said, "but I don't want any trouble. After Tío Balde had left, Papá asked me to come in and sit down so he could discuss something important with me.

"Alejandro, I think you know that Lorena has left and taken little Cleofas." Papá laid his wet bandana out on the table and folded it neatly. "Balde is very angry, and I'm afraid he may make problems with Lorena. He shouldn't go to Tres Zopilotes alone."

I nodded in agreement. Sometimes Tío Balde could get very angry and do crazy things.

"I need you to go with us tomorrow. I want you to help me keep Balde out of trouble." Papá shook his head and frowned. "This could be a serious situation, and I really need you to be with me."

"I'll go," I said. Papá had never before asked me for this kind of help. I felt he was at last treating me as if I was important to him. "Don't worry, Papá. I'll help you."

Papá arose from the table and did something that he didn't do very often. He patted me on the back. "Thank God I have a son that I can depend on." He turned and walked out of the kitchen.

Later that night, Mamá said that she knew that Papá had asked me to go with him and Tío Balde to Tres Zopilotes.

"Listen carefully, Alejandro. If you see little Cleofas, grab him quickly and bring him here."

"But, Mamá, do you think that that would be the right thing to do to Tía Lorena?" I was concerned with the feelings of a woman who had been kind to me.

"It'll be all right. Little Cleofas needs to be here with his brother and his father. Just do as I tell you."

Early the next morning, Tío Balde asked Mamá to care for Lito. Then Tío Balde, Papá, and I made the three-quarters of an hour trip down the river to Tres Zopilotes in Tío Balde's old pickup truck. Tres Zopilotes was a small dusty South Texas village like so many others at that time along the Rio Grande. It had a tree-lined plaza surrounded by a few businesses and some houses. The rest of the village was just a sprinkling of houses and outbuildings. The only paved street was a two-lane road full of potholes that ran beside the plaza.

Tía Lorena's sister lived in one of the houses facing the plaza. Tío Balde parked his pickup in front of the house and walked directly up to the door. Papá and I got out of the truck but didn't go up to the house. Tía Lorena's sister came to the door. She told Tío Balde in a loud voice that she had not seen Tía Lorena or little Cleofas and that Tía Lorena had left because Tío Balde was such a bad husband. She said that wives only leave husbands who mistreat them, and she was glad Tía Lorena had left. Then she slammed the door.

Well, that was the end of that. But, no, Tío Balde wasn't going to give up that easily. He had us get back into the pickup, and we drove away. Then he turned around and returned to the plaza, but parked the pickup on a side street next to a *cantina,* where it couldn't be seen from the plaza.

"Let's go in for a *cerveza, hermano,*" Tío Balde said. "And you, Alejandro, don't you want a soda pop?"

We walked into the dark, musty-smelling *cantina.* The place was deserted except for a bushy-headed bartender. Papá talked to him as I looked at some photos of Pancho Villa hanging on the wall. I really wanted something to eat, like one of the pickled pigs' feet that I saw in a jar on the bar, but I settled for a Delaware Punch. Tío Balde sent me out to the plaza so I could watch Tía Lorena's sister's house. He said that perhaps I might see Tía Lorena or little Cleofas because he was sure that they were there.

The plaza was deserted. I selected a shady spot on a wrought-iron bench and sat down to enjoy my Delaware Punch. The town was rather quiet except for a dog that was barking in the distance. Occasionally a cicada made its irritating buzzing noise from somewhere in the tree above me. I finished my Delaware Punch and got up to take the empty bottle back to the *cantina* when I saw a small boy come out of Tía Lorena's sister's house. It was little Cleofas, and he was alone. I remembered what Mamá had told me, and I quickly walked across the road and up to the child. He recognized me immediately and smiled. I glanced around to see if anyone was watching me. I saw no one.

"Do you want to see your father?" I asked.

Little Cleofas didn't respond.

"Do you want a Delaware Punch?" I asked as I held up my empty bottle.

He reached for the bottle, so I took him by the hand and started walking slowly toward the *cantina*. I looked back at the house and saw Tía Lorena watching us from a window. I thought it was strange that she was smiling at me. I expected to hear her open the door and call to me to stop and bring her child back. But no one came to the door and no one tried to stop me from walking away with the small boy.

As soon as Tío Balde saw me with his son, he hurried us into the pickup, and we sped out of Tres Zopilotes. Little Cleofas responded as a typical three-year-old child. He cried for his mother almost all the way back to Chicken Foot Farm.

Tío Balde's pleasure of having his two sons with him was short lived. He couldn't leave the young children at home alone, so he couldn't do much work on the farm. This made

Papá unhappy because he was paying him to work. Tío Balde decided to enlist my mother to care for his children. He came over one morning to where Mamá was scrubbing clothes in a washtub under the fresno tree. Abuelo Angel and I sat at the grinding stone where he was sharpening the kitchen knives. Tío Balde stood before Mamá with his straw hat in front of him and his eyes looking at his feet as he made his request.

Mamá didn't look up, but continued her chore. "I don't mind watching them occasionally, but I have enough family of my own to care for. And, I'm getting a little too old to have to do all the work that little ones require."

I looked at Mamá and thought I saw a slight smile on her face as Tío Balde walked away. With Abuela Luciana gone, there was no one left to turn to but Virginia and Tía Inocencia. They told Tío Balde that they absolutely would not care for his sons. This was very unusual, especially for Virginia. Tía Inocencia told Tío Balde that she was going to notify the sheriff to have the little boys put in an orphanage.

For about two weeks, Tío Balde tried doing his farmwork with his boys following behind him. When that didn't work too well, he tried doing his work at night while the boys were asleep in the house with Abuelo Angel. Besides not being able to see well in the dark, night work made my uncle tired and cranky.

A lot of the time the little boys hung around the kitchen, crying for something to eat, or just crying for no reason. Mamá and Virginia fed them, and hugged them, and wiped their runny noses. Even Abuelo Angel tended to some of the boys' needs.

I was surprised to see that Tía Inocencia was concerned about the little boys. She said she did not like the way that little Cleofas ran around the compound with nothing on his body but a dirty undershirt. She stopped Tío Balde outside the kitchen one night and shook her fat finger at him.

"It's a disgrace to this family that little Cleofas is always naked and dirty. You need to take better care of your children, or the orphanage will definitely come for them."

"But what can I do?" Tío Balde whined. "These children get so dirty, they need bathing almost every day. We're out of clean clothing, and Lorena took all of Cleofas's underwear with her." Tío Balde paused and then added in a lowered voice, "And worst of all, both boys cry a lot for Lorena. What can I do?"

Mamá, who had been observing this interaction, said to Tío Balde, "Maybe you should have been kinder to Lorena. Have you thought about that?"

He must have been thinking about it a lot because that same day he and his two sons went down to Tres Zopilotes and brought Lorena back home. I never heard another word about the episode, but I did notice that Tío Balde treated Tía Lorena better than he ever had before.

XIX

The Horse Rider

A buelo Angel had been correct about Toribio Tovar buying our mules; in fact, he bought both of them. Now I had only the milk cow to stake out for grazing on the grass along the barrow ditches. I staked her out in the mornings before going to school and went back for her in the late afternoons. It was in early May when I had gone to get the cow that I first saw the horse rider. She was coming across our field riding bareback on a pinto gelding and leading the two mules that Toribio had bought from Papá.

She must not have seen me in the tall grass until I raised my hand and yelled, *"¡Hola!"*

She appeared startled and unsure and quickly reined her gelding. I waved at her again, and she slowly started moving toward me. She wore a long, full skirt that allowed her to easily straddle the back of the animal. Her white blouse was stained and tattered, and she was barefoot. I scrutinized her and thought that she probably wasn't from this area.

"Who are you? And what are you doing coming across our land?" I moved closer to her.

I saw that she had a pretty face, and her black hair hung in two braids adorned with bright red ribbons. In her ears dangled long silver earrings that jiggled as she moved her head. I was intrigued by her looks.

She reined her gelding. "My name is Adriana Serna. I'm sorry. I didn't know this was your land."

"What are you doing with Toribio Tovar's mules?" I walked up to her.

"Don Toribio told me to stake his mules out here where the grass is tall. My father will come for them later. He works for Don Toribio."

"Where do you live?" I was surprised that Toribio had hired new help.

She pointed toward the *monte*. "We live in a small *jacal* on the north edge of the *monte*. It belongs to Don Toribio." Then she turned her head to the cow that was grazing nearby. "Is she yours?"

"Yes, I come for her every evening. The grass is very good here. You can stake the mules along here and the pinto, too, if you want."

She smiled at me and jumped off of her gelding and began staking the mules that were already grazing.

I pulled up the cow's stake and said, "Don't worry about coming across our land. It's alright." The cow and I started for home. I wanted so badly to turn and look back at her, but I didn't.

All the next day at school I thought of the girl on the pinto gelding and looked forward to seeing her again. I had trouble keeping my mind on my studies, but I knew that I had to pass all of my classes so I could graduate high school at the end of May.

During the remaining days of May, Adriana and I met several times along the barrow ditch. Sometimes I waited for her, but she never came. There were a few afternoons that Mr. Serna or Adriana's brother, Domingo, brought the mules. On those days, I didn't approach them but stayed away until they were gone. I felt disappointed and wondered why Adriana had not come. On the days that Adriana and I did meet along the barrow ditch, I enjoyed talking to her. Twice we lingered longer than we should have, and Domingo came looking for her.

One evening Abuelo Angel asked me, "Why is it taking you so long to bring in the cow? We need to milk her before dark."

I told my grandfather the truth, and I told him that I enjoyed talking with Adriana.

Abuelo Angel listened to me, then nodded and said, "I've met Mr. Serna and his son. They're a very humble family and probably won't stay much longer because I suspect that Toribio pays them very little."

But they did stay, and I was just getting brave enough to think of introducing myself to Adriana's father when he came to our kitchen doorway early on a warm summer morning. He had ridden the pinto gelding from the little hut where he lived. I noted that he appeared somewhat exhausted.

"Please help me. My son is dead, and I don't know what I should do."

"What's happened?" Papá motioned for Mr. Serna to come in.

"My boy had been sick for several days, and yesterday he ran high fevers. Then the convulsions came." Mr. Serna sank down on one of the benches. "He died during the night."

Mamá offered Mr. Serna coffee and food, but he said no and thanked her.

"Don Toribio told me he couldn't help me and that I should contact the county. I don't know where that is," Mr. Serna looked at Papá and then at Abuelo Angel. "I'm not from here. I have no money. What should I do about my son?"

"You should contact the county coroner, I'm sure," said Papá. "Don't worry about that, we'll help you."

Papá took Tía Lorena and Mamá to the Serna's hut to help prepare the boy's body for burial. Abuelo Angel and Tío Balde used some of the lumber left over from the construction of our new kitchen to make a simple coffin. When it was finished, Tío Balde and I loaded it onto the bed of my uncle's pickup. Abuelo Angel asked me to go with them to take the coffin to the Serna's. Virginia gave us bean tacos and *pan dulce* to take with us to give to the Serna family.

Upon arriving at the hut, I could understand why Abuelo Angel had said they were a very humble family. They had no furniture and no beds; the family slept on *petates* like the seasonal farmworkers that Papá hired occasionally. Adriana and her mother cooked outside on a grate over a small fire pit. On the grate, I saw a cast-iron kettle with its lid turned over to use as a *comal*. A blackened coffeepot was sitting on the ground nearby. Someone had made a small table out of citrus crates, and on it sat a few cups and tin plates.

As far as the *jacal*, it was an unlivable hovel. The floor was dirt, and the roof was almost nonexistent. Someone had tied a tarp over the top of the *jacal*, but that wouldn't have kept out even a gentle rain. There was a doorway, but no door. The entire structure looked as if it might fall over without provocation.

Inside the *jacal*, we found that Mamá and Tía Lorena had prepared Domingo's body and had wrapped it in a blanket. Papá and I brought in the coffin and put Domingo's body in it. We loaded the coffin in the back of the truck, and Papá and Mr. Serna took Domingo's body into town to make arrangements for a Christian burial. Adriana and her little sister, Susana, said nothing but sat on the ground with their heads bowed. I gave

Mrs. Serna the food that Virginia had sent, and then my family and I went home.

That night Abuelo Angel told Papá and me, "After seeing that these people are living so near the *monte* with so many rats and mice, I suspect that their son may have died of typhus."

Papá nodded in agreement. "I think we should help this family. I was thinking about giving them the lumber that we salvaged from the kitchen when it was knocked down."

Abuelo Angel nodded his head. "Yes, we can take it to them and help make the hut more livable. At least so they can be protected against the weather."

"That's a good idea," I said. I was afraid that I may have sounded a little too eager.

Abuelo Angel looked at me and smiled. "We'll take Alejandro to help. That way we'll get it done faster."

The sad occasion of Domingo's death was the beginning of a long-term friendship between Papá and Mr. Serna. They didn't know at the time that they would eventually become even more than friends.

XX

La Canícula

"Shredding is a better way," I had told Papá. "It's easier than your way of gathering the stalks by hand and burning them. I wish you would let us try shredding."

After he talked to Gordon about it, Papá agreed to try my method, and he bought a secondhand homemade shredder.

"Now, Alejandro, you will be the one to do all the shredding," Papá said.

"*Gracias*, Papá," I said and smiled.

"*No hay de qué*," Papá said and laughed.

So that's how I found myself on the tractor, during the dog days of summer, shredding the dried cotton stalks on an afternoon that was becoming unbearably hot and humid. I was having thoughts of going to the kitchen for something cool to drink when I saw Abuelo Angel waving for me to come in from the field. I left the shredding and joined him in the shade of the fresno tree.

"I think there's a storm coming," Abuelo Angel said and pointed to the east. "We're in the middle of *la canícula*, the season when dangerous storms can come out of the Gulf."

I had noticed earlier the large clouds that were building up in the east. Now they appeared to be getting darker and closer. "Do you think we'll have a bad thunderstorm?"

Abuelo Angel pulled at his long white mustache. "I think it may be worse, possibly *un huracán*. Look how still and quiet it is." Abuelo Angel lowered his voice. "Lots of sea birds have been flying over all day going west, and now our chickens are acting peculiar." Abuelo Angel cocked his head as if he were listening to something. "I feel it in my bones, Alejandro. We need to get ready for a hurricane."

Papá and Tío Balde had gone to town and hadn't returned yet. I began gathering tubs, buckets, and chairs from the yard and putting them in the bathhouse. Tío Erasmo called to me to come and help him cover his windows.

"The radio reports say we're in for a big one," Tío Erasmo said as he reached under his house for a piece of plywood. "I'm going to protect my windows."

"Don't take time for that," yelled Tía Inocencia when she saw Tío Erasmo and me pulling the plywood pieces from under the house. "Hurry up, Erasmo, get the truck loaded! I want out of here!"

Tío Erasmo dropped the piece of plywood and hurried into his house to begin bringing out the suitcases and boxes that Tía Inocencia had packed. Cándido, Roque, and I helped to load the big blue farm truck.

"We will stay at my in-law's house in Laredo until the storm is over," said Tío Erasmo. "You tell your father that I think he needs to get his family out too."

"We have no place to go, except to Tío Onécimo's in San Antonio. That's probably too far for Papá to want to go." I couldn't imagine Papá leaving the farm totally alone.

"Well, load up your pickup truck with food and water and go farther up the river. Get away from the coast." Tío Erasmo climbed into the driver's seat and started the truck. "And, if you don't leave, at least tie your house down." Tío Erasmo waved good-bye and drove away.

I found Virginia and Mamá in the kitchen. Mamá was making flour tortillas, and Virginia was preparing a large pot of coffee.

"Your grandfather thinks there's a bad storm coming, so we're getting some food prepared," said Mamá. She stopped long enough to wipe the perspiration from her face. "*Ay, Dios,* it's terribly hot in this kitchen today." Mamá wrapped a stack of tortillas in a cloth. "I'm certain your grandmother wouldn't have liked this kitchen either."

"Maybe I should use Tío Erasmo's plywood and cover the windows on our house," I said.

"I think you should cover the kitchen windows first. We need to protect this new kitchen the best we can." Mamá wiped her face again.

Virginia laughed and said, "Yes, we do need to protect it, because if something happens to this one, we won't get another one for years."

Mamá frowned at Virginia. "Don't laugh. Your father spent all of his money on new materials to build this one."

Virginia shrugged. "Well, nothing can happen to this one. It's so well made, and after all, we've already lost it two times." Virginia began pouring coffee into two vacuum bottles to keep it hot. "Surely it can't ever happen again."

I left to go get the plywood from under Tío Erasmo's house and saw Abuelo Angel coming across the yard carrying a bundle of thick rope. I helped him take the heavy bundle off of his shoulder. "I'm going to cover the kitchen windows with plywood," I said.

Abuelo Angel rubbed his shoulder and grimaced. "When you finish that, come help me bring the iron spikes from the equipment shed." He leaned against the fresno tree, breathing heavily. "I also need you to find the sledgehammer."

"Why do you want spikes and the sledgehammer?"

"To tie down the house." Abuelo Angel began laying pieces of the rope across the yard. "And don't leave the tractor and the shredder out in the field."

I rushed to bring the plywood from Tío Erasmo's house. I nailed the smaller pieces over the windows of my parents' house and the larger ones over the four windows of the new kitchen. By the time I had completed this task, Papá and Tío Balde had returned from town and were throwing ropes over the roof of our house. The ends of the ropes were being secured with the long iron spikes that were hammered deep into the ground. I wondered how those ropes could possibly keep a strong wind from whisking the little wooden house off of the few concrete blocks on which it sat.

As I was bringing the tractor and shredder to the equipment shed, the wind began to come in gusts. The huge bank of black menacing-looking clouds was moving closer to us. A few small dust devils skipped across the fields between us and Toribio's farm. I suddenly thought of the Serna family, and especially Adriana. How could they possibly stay safe in their little *jacal*, especially if it was in the path of a hurricane?

After securing the tractor, I found Papá and asked him what he thought about the safety of the Serna family. Although we had greatly improved their *jacal*, it was still not a strong structure. He told me to take his pickup and bring them to Chicken Foot Farm.

The wind was blowing stronger by the time I arrived at the Sernas'.

Adriana rushed out to the pickup. "My father says he thinks there's a bad storm coming. I'm afraid."

"Hurry, get everyone into the pickup. You and your family will stay with us."

Mrs. Serna, Adriana, and Susana crowded into the cab with me. Mr. Serna rode in the back with the few bundles that they were bringing. By the time we arrived back at Chicken Foot Farm, the rain was coming in squalls.

"Take them into our house," Papá yelled above the sound of the wind and rain. "I have to put out the fire in the cook-stove. We don't want to have the kitchen burn down again."

Abuelo Angel suggested that we should all wait out the storm in the parlor because it was on the west side of the house. In the parlor we had only the sofa and the horsehair chair, so most of the men and younger people sat on the floor. Adriana and Susana positioned themselves on the floor across the room from me.

The house trembled in the strong wind. The electrical bulb hanging from the ceiling began blinking off and on and soon went dark. Mamá lit two of our kerosene lanterns. I looked at Adriana and saw that she was looking at me and smiling. We didn't dare talk to one another in front of our parents. I smiled back, and she quickly looked away. I continued looking at her and realized how much I was attracted to her. In fact, I really liked her. She glanced back at me for a moment and smiled. The thought of sitting on the floor all night and looking at her in the dim light of the kerosene lamps pleased me.

The wind began to blow harder, and Cleofas and Lito moved in closer to me, one on either side. Mamá, Tía Lorena, and Mrs. Serna sat together on the sofa. They had been talking but had stopped now that the house was rattling and the wind was making a loud howling sound. Abuelo Angel sat in the big chair trying to find weather reports on his battery-powered radio.

"I've never seen anyone tie a house down," said Mr. Serna who had situated himself on the floor near Papá and Tío Balde. "But of course, there are no hurricanes where we come from."

"We've had a few bad ones here. We tied this very same house down in 1933," Abuelo Angel said and handed me the radio, apparently to let me find a station.

I had heard about the 1933 hurricane many times from my parents and my grandparents. I didn't remember the storm because I was very young and had slept through it, but I could picture in my mind what had happened. According to the story, the wind blew objects against the windows, shattering the glass panes. Rosa, Miguel, and I were the only ones that didn't get cut because Mamá had put us under the bed. Now that I had boarded the windows, I hoped that this time we would all remain safe from broken glass.

We had been in the parlor for about an hour when the wind began to really test the ropes. The roof seemed to intermittently lift and fall with loud banging sounds, and the wind continued to make an eerie howling noise. Occasionally, we could hear objects being blown against the walls of the house. The rain was being driven so hard by the wind that water had begun to come through the wall of the room on the east side of the house.

"Virginia, your bed is getting wet from the leaks." Papá said after he returned from checking the other two rooms.

"*Ni modo*, maybe I can get a new one if I'm lucky." Virginia shook her head and laughed.

Several hours later, when Adriana and I were playing our silly game of look, smile, and look away, I noticed that the wind had stopped blowing. Papá opened the outside door. There was not a sound to be heard. Papá took one of the lanterns and stepped out onto the porch. "I'm going out to see how much damage we've had."

"Be careful. If we've had a direct hit, remember that this is the eye." Abuelo Angel stood up. "The other side of the hurricane will hit us soon, and that may be the worst side."

Tío Balde and Mr. Serna joined Papá outside. The rest of us stood up and moved around to stretch our legs.

Papá and Mr. Serna soon returned.

"Most of the damage is broken tree limbs, and some of the outbuildings have roofs gone," Papá said as he tried to clean the mud off of his shoes.

Tío Balde stepped into the house. "The cow is not hurt. The dogs all came out from under the house with their tails between their legs. They're scared but alive."

"And my chickens?" said Mamá.

"I didn't check the chicken house," said Papá.

Virginia opened the last of the vacuum bottles and poured coffee into several cups. She passed the cups to Papá, Tío Balde, and Mr. Serna.

"Perhaps we should all have something to eat. I'm sure it's long past time for our evening meal." Mamá opened a small bundle and began to pass out bean tacos.

We had just finished eating when the wind and rain began again. Abuelo Angel had been correct about the back side of the storm being worse. The wind blew for hours without relenting. Our house shuddered and shook and bounced. When I thought the storm couldn't get any louder, we heard a terrifying sound as if a train were passing over our house. I felt the floor trembling under me. I heard the porch being ripped off of the house. Somehow the house stayed on its concrete blocks. Lito and Cleofas clung to me, and I held tightly to them until they both fell asleep. They were the only ones who were able to sleep that night.

By daylight the wind had subsided, but the rain continued to fall. One by one we slowly exited the house to view an unbelievable sight. Large tree limbs, pieces of lumber, roofs, and roof shingles were strewn all over the compound. Scattered among the debris were dozens of dead grackles and sparrows.

But worst of all, Abuelo Angel's house and kitchen were totally demolished.

"It came like a cyclone," said Abuelo Angel as he stood looking at the pile of rubble that had been the house that he had shared with Abuela Luciana for many years. "And now there's nothing left." He took his bandana from his pocket and wiped his eyes.

I walked over to Mamá and Papá. They were standing near where the kitchen had been. It appeared to have been picked up and slammed back down where it broke into thousands of pieces. Not even the cookstove was visible.

Mamá was crying. "Sigi, what shall we do now?"

"We'll build a new kitchen. I'm going to use cement blocks to build it this time. Nothing will destroy it." Papá put his arm around Mamá's shoulders.

"But our nice kitchen is gone," Mamá said.

"It was just a building, Ramona. We're still alive and we still have the land." Papá turned to me. "Just look, Alejandro," he said as he raised his arm and moved it in a sweeping motion, "This will all be yours someday."

His statement surprised me. "But I'm not your eldest son," I said.

"That doesn't matter. I can give my land to whomever I please."

Papá's apparent newfound attitude surprised me again later that day when I saw him looking through the pile of debris that had been my grandparents' house. Papá picked up something out of the rubble. It was a small white banner with one gold star. He wiped it off with his bandana, then carried it into the house and hung it in the parlor window.

Epilogue

Sometimes Adriana and I take our grandchildren to see what's left of Chicken Foot Farm. What used to be the family compound now lies under an overpass of a six-lane expressway. Our houses, outbuildings, and the cement-block kitchen have been replaced by paved streets, curbs and gutters, and massive cement pillars. Most of the farmland has been taken over by businesses and housing developments, and the *monte* was leveled to make room for a large mobile home sales lot, apartment complexes, and a Wal-Mart Super Center. Not far from the expressway the Fisher house still stands, dwarfed by large commercial buildings. Gordon Fisher lived there until his death a few years ago. I've heard that the house will soon be demolished.

Toribio Tovar's house has been gone for a long time. I recently saw a picture in the local newspaper of Toribio sitting in front of a big birthday cake. It was surprising that the staff at the nursing home where he lives got all 100 candles lit at one time.

Tío Balde and Tía Lorena moved to Tres Zopilotes where they bought the *cantina* on the plaza. According to Tío Balde, they're making lots of money and getting rich. Tío Erasmo and Tía Inocencia moved to California and lived there until my uncle died. I heard that Tía Inocencia went with Cándido to Alaska, where he has a good job operating large dirt-moving equipment.

My cousin Ubaldo became the most educated member of the family by earning a Ph.D. in education. He's a public school superintendent somewhere out in West Texas. As far as Miguel, he stayed in San Antonio, where he worked at the Martínez Mercantile and Grocery for a few years. Tío Onécimo finally had to close the little store because it wasn't making any money. Miguel found employment with a large grocery store chain, where he worked until he retired. We see him often because he comes down to our part of Texas to go bird watching along the river.

Sometime after the war was over, Ernesto's remains were sent home. He was buried with military honors at Fort Sam Houston National Cemetery in San Antonio. My sisters and I visit his grave at least once a year and place flowers in front of his plain white stone marker.

Virginia didn't marry Gordon Fisher or Pedro Ramos. Soon after Pedro came back from the war, he married another woman. I think it broke Virginia's heart. She never married, but stayed at Chicken Foot Farm tending to the needs of Abuelo Angel and my parents until their deaths. Virginia now lives in town with Rosa who was widowed by Manny's death in an oil field accident. I go almost every day to visit my sisters. We sit around the table in Rosa's kitchen drinking decaffeinated coffee and eating ginger pig cookies.

The other day, Virginia said something to me that made a shiver run up my spine. She said that when she travels the expressway, she feels a tingling surge running through her body as her automobile passes over our old family compound. She said that she thinks this would happen even if she had a blindfold over her eyes. I didn't tell her, but I've also experienced a weird sensation at the same spot on the expressway. I wish I could explain it, but I'm not sure I can. Perhaps it's just an overactive imagination. However, I prefer to believe that it's caused by the spiritual bonds that exist between individuals and the places that have enchanted them.

Also by Anne Estevis

Down Garrapata Road